Amuro pulled the trigger of his rifle and fired. The Elmeth started to swoop below him, but he had anticipated the maneuver and brought up the Gundam's left leg, smashing it into the Elmeth's prow. Under normal conditions what he had done would have appeared comical. His MS was humanoid, and he had in effect "kicked" the enemy. But his MS was also a weapon of war, and to be used as he saw fit.

The shock of physical contact reverberated through the Gundam cockpit, and Amuro saw the Elmeth shudder. And in the same instant he felt a powerful "force" bearing down on him simultaneously from both his front and rear. Could it be the Elmeth's remote units? Since he was attacking their mother machine, they were surely out to get him. In the "force" pressing on him, he could detect a single thought:

Kill him!

By Yoshiyuki Tomino
Published by Ballantine Books:

GUNDAM MOBILE SUIT:
Volume I: Awakening
Volume II: Escalation
Volume III: Confrontation*

*Forthcoming

Gundam Mobile Suit Volume II

ESCALATION

Yoshiyuki Tomino

Translated by Frederik Schodt

A Del Rey Book
BALLANTINE BOOKS • NEW YORK

A Del Rey Book
Published by Ballantine Books

Library of Congress Catalog Card Number: 90-91847

ISBN 0-345-35739-6

Manufactured in the United States of America

First Edition: November 1990

English-language map by Shelly Shapiro

CONTENTS

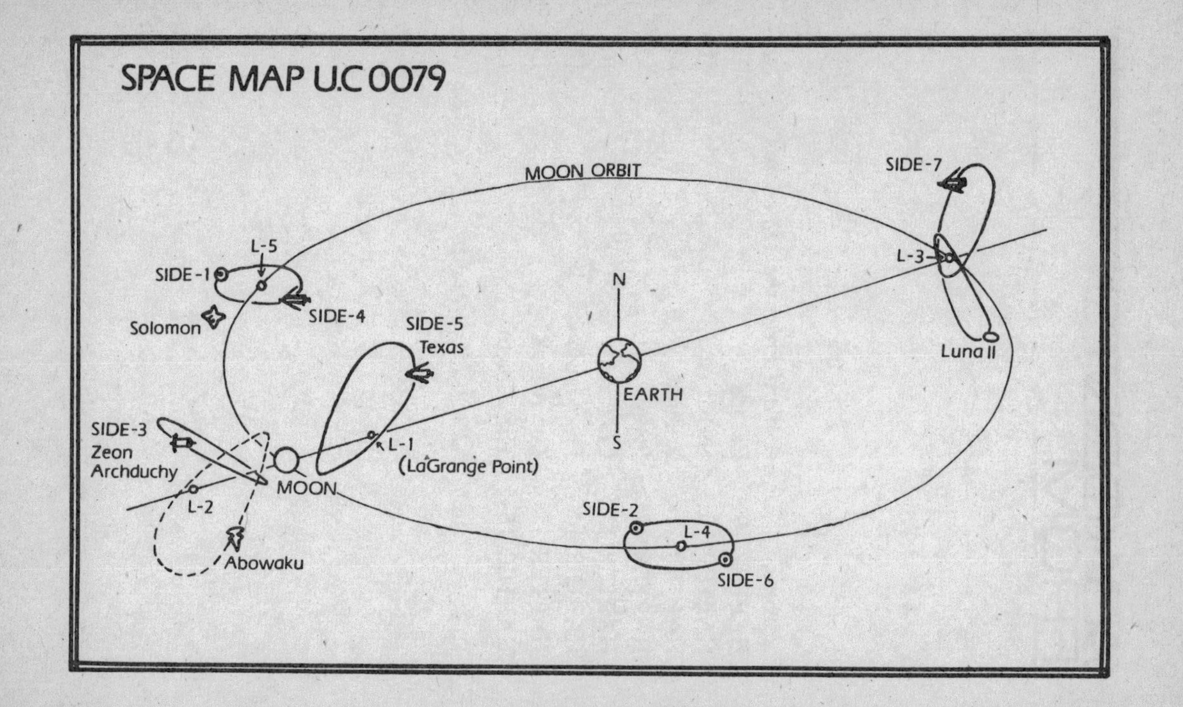
SPACE MAP U.C 0079
MOON ORBIT
SIDE-7
L-3
Luna II
L-5
SIDE-1
SIDE-4
Solomon
SIDE-5
Texas
N
EARTH
S
SIDE-3
Zeon
Archduchy
L-1
(LaGrange Point)
MOON
L-2
Abowaku
SIDE-2
L-4
SIDE-6

A WORD FROM THE TRANSLATOR

The Gundam Mobile Suit is no ordinary three-volume science fiction series. It is but one part of a fantasy universe and a social phenomenon of gargantuan proportions, Made-in-Japan.

GUNDAM began in 1979 as an animated television series, titled "Kidō Senshi Gundam," or "The Gundam Mobile Suit," but it had its roots in a long Japanese tradition of giant warrior robot animated TV shows for children (mostly boys). These stories were usually about struggles between good and evil forces, and adhered to formula plots—after an invasion by alien monsters or crazed robots, a young hero typically climbed into a "drivable" giant robot (a state-of-the-art model designed by his scientist father or uncle, who had been killed by the attackers), and then proceeded to save the world. As directors often lamented, because the shows were essentially commercials for toys based on the robot characters, they had to show robots in absurdly dramatic poses in as many action scenes as possible. The result was an endless series of hyped battles between thirty-stories-tall, sword-wielding, transforming warrior robots stomping through smashed cities.

Yoshiyuki Tomino, a veteran animation director, had long chafed at the constraints of the genre, and was determined to demonstrate that it had a greater potential. With GUNDAM, in 1979, he created a far more realistic storyline, and lavishly detailed both its characters and *mecha*, or high tech hardware. Influenced partly by Robert Heinlein's 1959 novel, *Starship Troopers*, he abandoned traditional Japanese robot concepts and made the ''Mobile Suit,'' a type of armored suit or piloted exoskeleton, the centerpiece of his story. He paid attention to the laws of physics and limits of believability, and he introduced characters with complex personalities that were difficult to pigeonhole as simply good or evil.

The first television series did not begin with high ratings, but it ended as a sensation, and marked the start of a GUNDAM decade in Japan. It also gained a near fanatical following among a much older audience group than would have normally been expected—many viewers were junior and senior high school, even college, students. The success of the first TV series thus led to a second in 1985, titled ''Z Gundam'' (Zeta Gundam), and then a third in 1986, titled ''Gundam ZZ'' (Gundam Double Zeta). The first TV series was reedited for theatrical release as three features, and in 1988 an original theatrical release, titled *Gundam Mobile Suit: Char's Counterattack* followed. Yet another feature is planned for 1991. In conjunction with TV broadcasts and theatrical features, a series of original animation videos, ''The Gundam Mobile Suit 0080'' has also been on sale since 1989.

Films are only one part of the GUNDAM universe. Toys are traditionally merchandised in conjunction with animation in Japan, and GUNDAM has been no exception. But instead of gaudily painted, sturdy robot toys for little boys, GUNDAM is famous for its beautiful scale models of the show's *mecha*, detailed with an unprecedented aura of "realism." These, too, have been a sensation. On one Sunday morning in 1982 nineteen young Japanese were injured in a near riot that broke out at a department store where crowds were vying to purchase the models. Nearly one thousand different types of GUNDAM plastic models have subsequently been produced, and over one hundred million have been sold—nearly one for every man, woman, and child in Japan.

Books are another component of GUNDAM. The original edition of the first three-volume series of GUNDAM novels was published in 1979 by Asahi Sonorama, and followed in 1987, by another, re-worked edition published by Kadokawa. Authored by Yoshiyuki Tomino, the creator and director of the animation shows, the novels have allowed him to develop the *Gundam* universe with even more detail and sophistication than possible in the animation. Appealing to an even older age group, the books have also been wildly successful. The original three-volume GUNDAM series (this one) has sold well over one million copies, as has a subsequent five-volume Z GUNDAM series. In addition, over one hundred different illustrated and special interest GUNDAM books have been marketed.

An entire generation of Japanese has been raised on GUNDAM stories and images, but the ultimate testimony to the concept's success is that there has even been a parody animation series created, called "SD (Super Deformation) Gundam." It, of course, has also been accompanied by heavy merchandising—miniaturized, comical versions of the original GUNDAM scale models have been the rage among young children since 1988.

This Del Rey edition of the Gundam Mobile Suit is an English translation of the 1987 Kadokawa edition of the first series of three novels. I have tried to be as faithful as possible to the original Japanese in my translation, while striving for an English structure that is as natural as possible. This may seem an easy task, but with a language as different as Japanese, it is not always so. Luckily, Yoshiyuki Tomino's epic is set in outer space, and most cultural and historical differences have been neutralized as a result, making the job of translator far easier, and giving the novels a truly international atmosphere. Careful readers, however, will occasionally note Japanese names and a uniquely Japanese flavor.

To hardcore U.S. GUNDAM fans a caution is due. In much of the English language promotional material that has emerged from Japan over the last decade, character names have not been transliterated into English in a unified fashion. I have therefore given priority to the original Japanese text, and some of the spellings I employ therefore differ from those popular in English language promotional materials and fanzines. For example, the name of Amuro Rey's arch rival is often written as "Char," whereas I have chosen "Sha," which is closer to the original.

GUNDAM has inspired countless imitators in Japan and set a standard for science fiction that few have equaled. And despite the fact that neither animation nor books have been officially introduced in the United States, GUNDAM has already had a major, albeit indirect, influence on the American SF-fantasy world, in terms of both character and *mecha* design. With the Del

Rey English language edition of the Gundam Mobile Suit, American SF fans can now finally read the original novels of the story they have heard so much about. But the GUNDAM universe is vast and still expanding and these novels are but a small peek into it. Hopefully they will soon be followed by many others.

Frederik L. Schodt

Several small nuclear explosions occurred, and the *Texas* colony began to self-destruct. Two Federation cruisers standing by outside, the *Saphron* and the *Cisco*, boldly ventured into the vast interior of the cylinder in a desperate attempt to rescue survivors from the *Pegasus*, a Federation assault landing ship, and the *Zanzibar*, a Zeon mobile cruiser. With luck they hoped to save at least thirty percent of the crews, but when the port modules on either end of *Texas* showed signs of rupturing out of the colony cylinder framework, they were forced to evacuate the area.

First the huge external mirrors normally used to reflect sunlight inside the colony were blown far into space. Then, when the final blast came, an enormous ring of light spread out from the colony, overtaking them and illuminating the drifting debris and fragments of other old colonies throughout the entire space shoal region known as the *Texas* Zone. The light was visible far away and was seen by both the forces of Rear Admiral Krishia Zavi of the Zeon Archduchy, and General Revil of the Earth Federation.

Lieutenant Commander Sha Aznable survived, but his Zak Mobile Suit was destroyed inside *Texas*, as was Zeon's state-of-the-art Mobile Armor, the Elmeth-Bits system, and its New Type pilot, Lala Sun. In the Elmeth, Lala had willed the remote controlled Bit units to attack and annihilate the pride of the Federation—the Gundam Mobile Suit—but had merely succeeded in inflicting heavy damage. Its pilot, young Ensign Amuro Rey, managed to flee the narrow confines of the colony in the Gundam's escape capsule, the Core Fighter. After achieving inertial speed, he soared through the danger zone and made a beeline for open space.

"These gizmos actually work . . ."

G-i-z-m-o-s. If the power failed on a Core Fighter, Amuro's instructor, Lieutenant Ralv, always used to say, its instruments would be about as useful as sunglasses in a cave at midnight—they would let one know if one were facing front or back, but that was it. To survive in space, *real* pilots relied on their eyes and their gut instincts.

". . . if the power fails, your instruments are as useful as sunglasses in a cave at midnight . . ."

How nostalgic the words now seemed.

"Lieutenant . . . look . . . the gizmos are working . . . Look how well the Core Fighter's made . . ."

He knew he had performed the right check procedures before escaping from *Texas*. The *Zanzibar* and the *Pegasus* had both blown their main engines and the Elmeth had been destroyed, and in the ensuing explosions the Gundam's main fuselage had begun to melt. He had instinctively activated the Core Fighter escape mechanism, but he wondered if some residual consciousness from Lala Sun might not have affected his judgment, even his mind. He remembered the colony walls flashing by on either side the instant his Core Fighter had exited *Texas*. He remembered the blurred shape of either the *Saphron* or the *Cisco*. He remembered seeing the actual moment of escape and the system operating as it was supposed to. And he remembered Ralv's comments about the instruments . . . But that was all.

Amuro Rey sank into fatigue-induced unconsciousness, but among his feverish thoughts there gradually appeared another, more assertive awareness. His deep subconscious was awakening; normally dormant functions of his cerebral cortex, now activated, were rising to the conscious level of his mind.

Lala . . . What happened? It was a ten- or twenty-minute encounter . . . and it all happened so fast . . . You showed me so much . . . But there's something that bothers me. There's something that bothers me terribly. We were virtual strangers. Absolute strangers. You weren't supposed to mean anything to me . . . How could we possibly have understood each other so well?

Is it because you were a New Type? A new human? Someone supposed to symbolize mankind's potential for a universal "renaissance"? And me? I may have better than average intuition, but I hardly think I'm a real New Type—I'm hardly some sort of new species that's going to transform humanity. Frankly, I don't believe that stuff for a minute. Lala, the whole thing's crazy. I don't know you any better than my childhood friend Fra Bow, or even Saila Mas, but our minds seem to fuse, Lala . . . to resonate . . . It felt as if we both glimpsed a way mankind could possibly evolve . . . But wait . . . no

. . . maybe it wasn't just us . . . Maybe it really was *part of that universal awakening people talk about, the new human renaissance that's supposed to happen someday . . .*

It makes me exhausted just to think about all this . . . I'm tired. I don't need anything now. I'm just going to sleep. That's all I want—to sleep . . . to sleep . . . The whole thing was too painful . . . I know you felt the same despair I did. Look what happened to us . . .

The next step in Amuro's awakening was triggered by anger.

Why, Lala? . . . Why were you on Sha's side?

That alien presence I felt . . . that presence that interrupted us when we first met in the docking bay of the Texas *colony port module . . . That was Sha Aznable, wasn't it, Lala? I felt static*—painful *static. But the expansion in awareness we were experiencing then . . . the leap in our ability to understand each other . . . it was incredibly powerful even if it was interrupted by hatred or an awareness of danger . . . Was it some sort of "thought transmission"? I know we're not the only ones capable of this . . . I'm sure we're not . . . But something still bothers me. Lala, why were you in love with Sha? Why were you on his side? Just because you love him? It seems beneath you, Lala . . . You must have been deluding yourself . . . To tell you the truth, I find it hard to believe . . . Nothing makes sense . . .*

Ensign Amuro Rey was comatose, and his thoughts were a series of illogically structured overlapping ideas that slid through his brain over and over again. The eight-meter-long Core Fighter carrying him continued in inertial flight, with no destination logged, streaking past the outer reaches of the *Texas* shoal zone toward the beckoning stars of an expanding universe. The ball of light from the exploding *Texas* colony behind it, once bright as a star between Earth and the moon, was slowly fading from sight. The little craft had used up almost all of its fuel in escaping from *Texas* and now had only enough left for a few attitude corrections with its vernier rockets. The soft glow of its instrument panel testified to the fact that it continued to function, but in reality the only operation regularly executed was an intermittent oscillation of a 360-degree identification laser-sensor. And the time limit on the pilot life-support system was slowly running out.

After leaving Luna II, the Federation fleet led by General Revil had headed toward Zeon's frontline moon base, *Granada*, arriving at the third combat line above it around the same time Amuro Rey's ship, the *Pegasus*, was destroyed in the conflagration inside *Texas*. The surviving ships in Amuro's unit, the 13th Autonomous, somehow managed to link up with other Federation units and execute their assigned feint maneuver, approaching *Granada* counterclockwise against the plane of the ecliptic while the main force closed in from the opposite direction. When all fleets reached their assigned stations, Revil's Magellan-class flagship, the battleship *Drog*, used a series of laser signals and rocket flares to transmit the following code to all ships in the armada:

BUTTERFLIES IN THE DESERT.

With these words the Federation Forces finally received their long-awaited instructions: to attack and occupy *Granada*. It was not going to be easy.

The Federation armada was huge, but its size hid the limitations in its actual fighting capability. The fleet led by General Revil was grouped around the space carrier *Trafalgar* and consisted of two battleships, seventeen *Coral*-class heavy cruisers, twenty *Salamis*-class regular cruisers, and sixty-five Public attack ships. Vice Admiral Karel's detachment was grouped around the space carrier *Garibaldi* and consisted of one battleship, seven heavy and eight regular cruisers, and thirty Public attack ships. Both the *Garibaldi* and the *Trafalgar* each carried sixty Cosmo fighters, for a combined total of 120.

In the old days an armada with so many Cosmo fighters would have been more than adequate for the task at hand, but Cosmo fighters had been designed for the radar age. Widespread use of Minovski particles had made radar ineffective and rendered former tactics obsolete. Instead of old-style hit-and-run dogfights over immense distances, true close-quarter combat had become the norm. Even homing missiles were nearly useless. When the Zeon Archduchy had developed its Zak model Mobile Suit, they had gained an overwhelming advantage. The Earth Federation Forces had continued to manufacture and deploy Cosmo fighters only because they had no choice; their development and production of Mobile Suits had lagged too far behind that of Zeon.

Unlike Zaks, most Mobile Suits carried by ships in the Federation armada were still relatively primitive. There were ninety of the VX-76 model—an early MS prototype nicknamed ''Bowls'' because of their rounded shape. They lacked legs but had vernier jets in a 360-degree configuration for attitude control and had a pair of rudimentary manipulator arms. The arms were incapable of holding anything as sophisticated as a beam rifle, but a hyperbazooka was built into the prow section. In addition, there were forty GM model Suits, a mass-produced version manufactured while the Gundam and Gun Cannon were still in the prototype stage. Instead of the stereobinocular design of the Gundam's head, the GM had a simplified glass front panel for a broader field of vision. And it had reinforced armor.

When General Revil issued the final burst of laser code from the *Drog* to the rest of the armada to initiate the attack, he chose the words "Tora tora tora"—the same phrase used in another age by the Imperial Japanese Navy when it had attacked Pearl Harbor and ushered in World War II on Earth. Although General Revil did not lack conviction in the justness of his cause and his certain victory, his choice of the words was a gross error bound to elicit criticism from future military historians. Japan was an upstart Far Eastern nation that without warning had suddenly attacked a territory of the superpower of the day, the United States of America, yet had eventually lost the war, at least technically. It would have been far more appropriate to use "Overlord" or "Neptune," names which the true victors in that conflict had used in their Normandy campaign.

The main Federation Force under General Revil's command accelerated to maximum combat speed and was followed 8,500 kilometers to the rear by Vice Admiral Karel's detachment, which entered moon orbit from an angle of sixty degrees and began descending toward *Granada*. The route of attack for the fleets had led through two difficult space shoal regions filled with the remnants of former colonies: *Texas* Zone and the area where Side 1 had formerly existed. By taking advantage of the cover this debris provided and by scattering a heavy concentration of Minovski particles to render enemy radar useless, the armada had been able to approach the third combat line above *Granada* without being detected. But from that point on it was necessary to use brute force. Using laser search beams, the Zeon defenders on *Granada* had already detected the armada and had gathered their forces in near the moon base. They were prepared to make a major show of resistance.

Rear Admiral Krishia Zavi, the commander of the *Granada* moon base, was worried.

"Still no further word on reinforcements from Supreme Commander Gren?" she asked the vice admiral next to her.

"Er . . . no, Your Excellency," he replied. "I've been trying to get word from our *Abowaku* space fortress for the last three days, but they keep saying they can't spare any forces until they know Revil's exact route of attack." Technically, the flag officer outranked Krishia, but he had to be circumspect. She was the eldest daughter of Archduke Degin Zavi, the nominal ruler of Zeon, and thus had absolute decision-making authority as far as he was concerned.

Krishia tugged on her veil-like mask. "Well, what about Dozzle on *Solomon*? Revil's obviously going to ignore *Solomon*. Have Dozzle muster his forces and attack him from the rear!" Her mask was made of a rubberized material that fit like a second skin, but she normally wore it down around her neck like a scarf, raising it above her nose only before going into battle. She was a woman of considerable vanity who liked to pretend it helped preserve her complexion, but in reality she hated the smell of battle. It was also true, ironically, that in the past the only time she had not worn it in battle, a supposedly inactive shell had exploded, killing a soldier next to her and overpowering her with the stench of death.

The vice admiral lied in response to Krishia's query. "I've already asked Dozzle, too, Your Excellency . . ." Then he took his leave.

And then it happened. The sixty-five Federation Public attack ships under General Revil's command blanketed the space over *Granada*, firing missiles that emitted a powerful electromagnetic field capable of diffusing enemy beams. It was an extension of the same technology used in radar-absorbing Minovski particles. The field remained effective for several minutes, and although incapable of diffusing 100 percent of all beams fired from the ground, for all intents and purposes the particles in it neutralized and scattered the consolidated electrons that made up the attacking beams. *Granada* was thus forced to abandon its beam cannon defense and resort to barrages of antiair weaponry using conventional explosives.

First, sixty Public attack ships slipped through *Granada*'s defensive fire and attacked the base with air-to-ground missiles. Then, while the *Salamis*-class Cosmo cruisers in the Federation fleet's vanguard engaged their Zeon *Musai*-class rivals in skirmishes, the ninety Federation VX-76 Bowls, supported by GMs, broke through *Granada*'s southern defense perimeter.

Simultaneously, Vice Admiral Karel's forces attacked the eastern perimeter of the base.

Because the Zeon ships defending *Granada* had been dispersed in local space, they were forced into a purely defensive role for the first thirty minutes of the assault wave. But then Rear Admiral Krishia Zavi, who was in charge, made a quick decision.

"Give the order to retreat!" she commanded. "But let it be known this doesn't mean Revil's beaten us. Tell headquarters *Granada* was lost because Gren vacillated in sending reinforcements. One more division and we could have easily repulsed the enemy!"

Thus absolving herself of all blame, Krishia boarded the *Zanzibar*-class Mobile Cruiser *Swamel* and abandoned *Granada*. Under normal Zeon military tradition, she would have been required to defend the base to the death, but both she and her brother, Supreme Commander Gren Zavi, had agreed in advance on a secret fallback plan. And in reality, her immediate decision was influenced less by this plan than by the emotions of the moment—by a burning desire to live and eventually confront Gren.

On the Federation side, the conquest of *Granada* was only part of a much larger strategy. The captured base gave their forces a beachhead on the back of the moon from which to attack the heartland of the Zeon Archduchy. Appropriately, they renamed it *FS*, or *First Step*.

A high-pitched sound stabbed through the darkness, expanded, and then suddenly transformed into a flash of light. It was not a horrifying flash, such as might accompany a nuclear explosion, but the gentle brilliance of a flare in blackness, the type of light that penetrated to the corners of the mind and then quickly faded into nothingness. Every time a sound arose from the distance, the light would flare in the darkness again. It was like the light a new life might encounter on emerging from a long period of gestation in the womb.

Amuro Rey's consciousness was slowly awakening.

Why, of course . . .

Mother, you were really unlucky . . . I know you were one of the privileged few to obtain permission to live on Earth. And I know it was mainly 'cause Dad was a well-known Side architect. But living on Earth spoiled you. It made you unable to adjust to the idea of living in space . . . and it made you refuse to join us . . . I wish you could have joined us . . . I don't know anything about marriage, but couples are supposed to help each other, right? Maybe Dad didn't love you enough, Mother. Maybe he really just lived to build more Sides in space, and maybe he treated you like his personal maid, or something . . . But Mother . . . what about me? I was your son! I was involved in all this, too . . .

I remember it as clear as day. I was five, and it was fall. October 28, to be exact. That's when Dad took me away from you . . . You kissed me on my left cheek. And I started to hate you. I didn't want to be a little boy anymore. I wanted to be a grown man. I hated Dad, too. I hated Dad for not being nicer to you. But if you had kissed me for just a few more seconds, Mother, I would have loved you. You were so stiff and formal . . . It made me think it was better to be with Dad . . . Why couldn't you come with us into space, Mother? Was it just because you didn't like the idea of living there? Or were you in love with another man?

You were, weren't you? That's why I left with Dad and didn't cry . . .

Another flare of light followed a far-off high-pitched sound. For a minute it seemed to Amuro that it was Lala Sun's voice . . . But then he could not hear it anymore . . .

The first sound Amuro heard was that of someone chuckling. It seemed to continue forever, but he could also make out the words, *"You mean the kid?"* He had no idea what was so funny, but in the process of trying to figure it out he began to regain consciousness. It helped, perhaps, that the voice belonged to a woman. It had a rather suggestive sound and was infinitely more pleasant than the gruff tone of the man who interrupted her. His words were hard to understand, and merely part of a whispered conversation in the darkness.

"Why not?" said the woman, giggling, but using a different tone. *"Don't you think he's kind of cute?"*

"Because we have rules against it . . ." The man seemed to be cautioning the woman against something.

Amuro tried to open his eyes and watched a light fixture directly above him gradually come into focus. It was a type of light he had seen a lot of in the last two years—a fluorescent panel covered with the protective mesh favored on military spacecraft.

I wonder if this is a military ship? he thought as his conscious mind began to reassert itself. He blinked several times. Aware of a woman's presence, he felt a little shy, but he wanted to know where he was. He tried moving his body for the first time, and a face peered down at him, blocking the light.

"Can you hear me?" The voice that sprang from the lips was bright and unaffected.

"Yes," he answered hoarsely. For a moment he wondered why he had replied so readily. He had no way of even knowing, after all, if the woman was from the Earth Federation. But any resistance faded with the sight of her smile.

"You've been asleep a long time," she said, "but you should be all right now. It must have been rough . . ." Then, turning from Amuro, she called for a doctor.

Amuro liked the way her jaw looked when she spoke.

She turned back toward him again. "Understand everything I say? My name's Kusko Al. Kus-ko-Al. You're on the *Kasetta III*."

"Kusko Al? Are you the one who rescued me?"

"Well, quite frankly, Ensign," she said with a toss of her long chestnut hair, "I don't know if 'rescue' is the right word or not. Our transport just happened to be the first to spot you, that's all."

"Thanks . . . I think I'm getting sleepy again . . ."

"You should rest, then, Ensign. You're safe now."

Amuro began sliding into sleep once more, but before losing all consciousness he heard a doctor enter the room and exchange words with Kusko Al.

". . . because he's an officer in the Federation Forces . . ."

The way it was said gave Amuro a vague sense of unease. But he trusted his own instincts. He detected no basic danger. And then he blacked out.

Later, Amuro would remember only a dream of his mother, Kamaria Rey. She was still living near his old home on Earth, but the war had involved her, too. She was lying naked in bed, wearing a Red Cross armband, next to a man he had never seen. Amuro, wearing his pilot suit, was standing and staring at both of them. He felt strangely dispassionate, but since his mother was married to his father, he wondered why she felt no shame.

"You shouldn't wear a cross on your bare arm like that, Mother," he said. *"It doesn't seem right, somehow."*

His mother's eyes showed no sign of anger, but her lips formed a little smile that seemed to say he was an unwelcome interruption.

It's your life to do as you please, Mother, but you ought to listen to your son once in a while.

He turned from her and the man and began walking away. His pilot's suit seemed heavier than ever. His boots had lead in their soles, and with each step they felt heavier and heavier. Five . . . six . . . seven steps . . . twelve, thirteen . . . when he reached twenty-three, he was no longer able to raise his feet off the ground. And then it happened. From his mother's bed in the shadows behind him came a scolding voice.

"What an ungrateful child you are! I didn't raise you to talk like that to me!"

"What to you mean by 'raise,' Mother? You didn't raise me! Even Dad was too busy with his work to raise me! I raised myself!"

Amuro was not really sad when he said it, but he wept anyway.

Then he was hundreds of kilometers away from his mother, but she came running naked after him, her hair all disheveled.

"Don't come near me!" he yelled, trying to flee. *"You're unclean!"*

He began running again, but the more he ran, the more leaden his feet became. He donned his pilot helmet and activated the sun visor in an attempt to block out all sight of her, but when he did, the sound of his labored breathing became a roar in his ears. *"Help! Help! I can't breathe!"* he screamed, groping desperately with both hands at the surroundings he could no longer see.

Then someone's hand took his. It was warm, and he somehow knew it belonged to the blond communications recruit who had been with him on the *Pegasus*. *"Saila, is that you?"* he asked.

"Ensign! Ensign!"

At the sound of the words Amuro's eyelids fluttered open. It was not Saila but Kusko Al. His guard instinctively up, he cursed himself for having fallen asleep again without verifying his rescuers' real identity.

"Thanks," he said, smiling. "I feel better now . . ."

At Amuro's confident reply, Kusko Al tossed her long chestnut hair again and smiled. But Amuro detected another, wavering thought behind her surface expression and sensed danger. She responded to him too quickly, too precisely, as if she already knew too much about him. *What am I feeling?* His mind began groping for an answer, but he tried to tone down his impulses. He would have to be careful. He knew nothing about her, and it would be better to feign ignorance if there were a threat.

"I was dreaming," he said. "It was frightening. And it was obscene . . ."

"Obscene?" Her pretty gray eyes narrowed as she stared down at him.

It worked! he exulted. The word "obscene," with all its physical implications, had caught her off guard. He had pierced her emotional barriers and aroused her basic feminine curiosity.

"My mother was sleeping with another man," he said.

Kusko Al was at a loss for words. The peach-fuzzed, innocent-looking young ensign in front of her was certainly not yet twenty, yet he spoke in a self-confident manner that belied his youth. No ordinary Federation pilot would speak in such casual terms about his mother to a virtual stranger. He was either an utter fool or . . .

"You've been through some hard times, Ensign," Kusko said. "You'd better forget the nightmares . . ."

"Thanks. I'd like to speak to the ship's captain if I may. Would you call him for me?"

With the aid of the doctor, Amuro checked himself, going from the top of his head down his neck and back to his tailbone. He was all in one piece, and he felt no pain. For a moment he wondered if his memory was intact, but then he remembered what he wished he could forget—the entire battle on *Texas*. What of his fellow crew members on the *Pegasus*? What had happened to them? It was too painful to think further, so he brought his attention back to Kusko, in front of him. She put down an intercom phone and turned to him.

"The captain will be here to see you any moment, Ensign."

"Thanks, I appreciate it."

He gingerly raised himself up on his elbows. Luckily, the *Kasetta*'s artificial gravity was only one-third that of Earth, for when he moved he felt enormous fatigue throughout his body, especially in his joints. He had worn his pilot suit too long.

"Where's this ship headed?" he asked.

"Side 6. We're scheduled to dock at Balda Bay. But be careful when you move like that. You okay?"

He could not tell if the concern expressed was real or merely a technique to get him to let down his guard, but the tone of her voice had suddenly changed.

"I'm fine. It wasn't a direct hit. By the way, what happened to my capsule?"

"Your 'capsule'? You mean that thing that looks like a light plane? It's moored on the ship's deck . . ."

Amuro said nothing. He knew he had made a major mistake in letting them get hold of his Core Fighter intact. He had referred to it as a capsule because he did not yet know who Kusko Al really was and needed to hide its true function from her. The "escape capsule" was far more than it seemed. It could operate as the Gundam's cockpit module, but when configured independently, the dozens of vernier jets on the winglike protrusions on its top, bottom, and sides made it highly maneuverable; it was called a Core Fighter because it could also function as a fighter. The problem was that there were several exposed joints on its external skin—joints that connected it to the Gundam's control system.

An expert seeing those joints would instantly realize what the capsule's function really was.

An unknown ship picked me up while I was unconscious . . . For Amuro, the unthinkable had happened. What would he do if his rescuers were really flying a Zeon flag and his Core Fighter had already fallen into enemy hands?

As Amuro watched, the door to the room opened and in walked an older man, with deep wrinkles around his eyes. The gold braid on his uniform suited him well and implied that he was the ship's captain. He was followed by another man in his mid thirties who appeared to be some sort of aide. While pondering the second man's role, Amuro stood up and saluted and noted for the first time the pain in this right upper arm.

"Ensign Amuro Rey, of the Earth Federation Forces' 13th Autonomous Corps. Thanks for rescuing me."

"You're more than welcome, Ensign. I'm Famira Ashul, the skipper of this ship, and this is Isfahan, my aide."

While nodding in greeting to both of them, Amuro indicated with his eyes to the captain that Kusko should leave. A perceptive man who seemed to be aware of the ways of the world, he immediately understood.

"Kusko," he asked, "would you mind leaving us alone for a minute?"

With a smile in Amuro's direction, she left.

Amuro addressed the captain. "I have two questions, sir."

"Fire away, Ensign."

"First, I need to dispose of the escape capsule you

found me in. Can you do it for me? Second, what is to become of me?"

"Relax, Ensign. Since your capsule is already tethered to the deck of the *Kasetta*, we cannot, unfortunately, allow you to dispose of it yourself. But the *Kasetta*'s registered to Side 6, so when we arrive your capsule will be handled according to the terms of the Neutrality Act that Side 6 has signed with the Earth Federation. That means that after going through immigration inspection at Balda Bay it will be turned over to the Federation consulate. As for yourself, we'll hand you over to the Federation consulate, too."

"That creates a problem for me, Captain . . ."

"Well, I'm sorry, Ensign, but regulations are regulations. Had you first abandoned your capsule and then requested rescue, the means of disposal would be your prerogative. But at this point the capsule is technically our cargo."

"How do you have it tethered?"

"Shall I show you, Ensign?"

"Captain Famira," the aide ventured, "er . . . are you sure it's all right?"

"The ensign used to own the capsule," the captain snapped. "We have no reason to refuse his request . . ." Then, to Amuro: "Think you can walk?"

Lift-grips were used in weightless areas of the *Kasetta III* to transport crew members. Handholds moving on guide rails built into the ship's walls, they could transport a single person at speeds of two to seven meters per second, but it took quite a knack to use them. One had to start "swimming" horizontally parallel to the grips and then grab on to one with the right arm to be pulled along. In places where there was a break in the guide rails, transfers were tricky. It was necessary to slow down two or three meters in advance, minimize all inertial movement, and then—after double-checking the position of the next grip to be grabbed—make the body swim straight toward it through the air. Accidentally bending a knee would create a different movement vector and make the connection impossible.

Amuro hadn't used a lift-grip for weeks. He grabbed the third grip after Captain Famira, following Isfahan the aide and Kusko Al. For the first time he noticed Kusko's shapely figure. She was wearing denim pants, and turned and smiled broadly at him.

"You can see your capsule out the hatch window over there, Ensign," Captain Famira said.

Amuro's view was blocked by the captain's enormous rear end in front of him, but he took his hand off the grip and let himself float up by the man's left side. Sure enough, through the thirty-centimeter-square hatch window he could see the expanse of the ship's upper deck and, on the starboard side, his Core Fighter tethered with wire cables. The canopy was bent, and the right wing had almost been destroyed. The fuselage seemed to have cracks in it.

While checking his craft visually through the narrow window, Amuro also scanned as much of the *Kasetta*'s outer deck as he could. In the shadow of a container on the left side of the deck he saw several people dressed in Normal Suits—the term used to describe space suits ever since Mobile Suits had been developed. Since the ship was a transport soon to dock at Side 6, there was nothing intrinsically odd about a few workers outside, but the fact that there were so many of them and that they were in the same area of the deck where his Core Fighter was tethered confirmed his worst fears. They were either Zeon military men or somehow connected to the enemy, he concluded. And one of them might already have entered his Core Fighter cockpit.

Pretending to be greatly relieved, Amuro turned to Famira and smiled broadly. "I can't thank you enough, Captain. I can't tell you what it means to me to be able to tell my superiors in the Federation that my capsule's right next to me."

"Well, I frankly feel as relieved as you do, Ensign. As soon as we disembark on Balda Bay, someone from the Federation Forces normally comes to interrogate us. It'll make it a lot easier for me if someone like yourself can vouch for us."

Amuro smiled in response.

"If the Federation consulate requests it," the captain continued, "I'm sure Side 6 will turn over your capsule right away."

"How long does it normally take to clear customs on Side 6?"

"With luck, two days. Without it, five days to a week. You've got to be prepared for the worst. Bureaucrats are the same all over the solar system . . ."

Amuro gazed out the hatch window again, and over the ship's prow he saw two bright lights in space in the distance. They were clearly Side 6 colonies, and one, he deduced, must function as a port—Balda Bay. A military ship could reach it in fifteen minutes, but the *Kasetta* was a transport and would take another two hours.

"Take a look at this monitor, Ensign," Kusko said, pointing at a screen next to her. Like most space ships, the transport had remote-control external security cameras monitoring its outside decks, giving Amuro an even better look at his Core Fighter. The system worked well, and the screen showed a high-resolution view of the

Core Fighter from above. When the cameras zoomed in for a close-up, shadows cast by the blazing sun were displayed with the proper exposure, and even details such as individual welds in the armor plating were clearly visible. Thankfully, there were no Normal Suited shapes meddling in the cockpit. But he sensed that not all was well.

He commented with veiled sarcasm, "The *Kasetta*'s certainly well equipped to handle my capsule . . ." Isfahan's eyes flashed angrily, and he knew the nuance behind his remark had registered. He looked back at the screen.

As a neutral territory aligned with neither the Earth Federation nor the Zeon Archduchy, Side 6 had been spared the ravages of the war, but its government leaned heavily toward Zeon. Its president, Rank Kiprodon, was widely rumored to be collaborating with Krishia Zavi. Amuro sensed, moreover, that the *Kasetta III* was in the enemy camp. And he also sensed that were it not for Captain Famira's personal goodwill toward him, he would certainly have been treated as a prisoner of war. But where, he wondered, did Kusko Al fit into all this?

"Thanks for your help," Amuro said to the captain. Then he started to grab on to a lift-grip. He knew the aide was secretly laughing at him, so he deliberately turned to Kusko Al and said, "Mind telling me where I can get some coffee around here?"

"If you'd like," she said flirtatiously, "I'll bring some to you in your quarters, Ensign . . ."

"You . . . you would?"

"Sure. You mind?"

The conversation was a ploy. Amuro had asked Kusko

Al because he wanted Isfahan to think he was personally attracted to her, and the strategy seemed to work—Isfahan smiled a thin smile as if to say, "Good luck, sucker . . ." But what really surprised Amuro was that although he had decided to use Kusko Al as a diversion, she seemed to have sensed his intention and even tried to help him. For a second he wondered if she might be a New Type. Unlike Lala Sun and Sha Aznable, he felt no spark of intuitive understanding with her. *I'll just have to see what develops and act as naturally as possible,* he thought, resolving to keep his guard up.

As a cargo ship, the *Kasetta III* had a rather rudimentary self-service mess hall with about twenty tables. A large counter protruded from the kitchen to the hall, with trays and utensils piled on it. Coffee was served from a coin-operated vending machine stuck against the far wall near the counter.

"Well, what'll it be?" Kusko asked.

"How about some mocha mandarin-flavored espresso?" Amuro asked, looking up at her bright gray-tinted eyes. She was a tad taller than he was.

"Let's not be too picky, Ensign," she bantered as she deftly filled two cups.

After moving over to a table beside the vending machine and sitting down, he asked her, "Do you understand my situation?"

"No, not totally, but the worried look on your face gave me a pretty good idea of what's going on. One thing's for sure. You'd never make a good spy."

Amuro chuckled and took a sip of some of the worst coffee he had ever experienced.

"I have to get my capsule off the *Kasetta III*, Kusko,"

he said. "If it's inspected on Side 6, my neck's on the line."

"That's what I thought. But if you're going to do something, you'd better hurry. We're docking at Side 6 soon."

"Soon?"

"Soon. Want me to help you, Ensign?"

She looked straight at him when she said this, and her gray eyes flashed. She had the ability to establish rapport instantly with men, and the positive first impression she gave off must have unhinged more than a few. What was it about her, Amuro wondered, that enabled her to do that? Perhaps, he thought, it was her absolute confidence in her own femininity.

Several minutes later they were standing in front of a desk manned by the crewman in charge of the ship's Normal Suit locker. Kusko Al turned and deliberately said to Amuro, "I feel like taking a walk. Want to join me for a look at the Side 6 colonies from outside the ship? We dock in thirty minutes, so we have to be back inside within ten." Then, turning to the young crewman and keeping a straight face, she said, "We just want to take a souvenir photo. No problem, right?"

Sure enough, after cautioning them to observe the time limit strictly, he handed over two Normal Suits.

From deck of the *Kasetta III* Amuro could clearly see all eight colonies that constituted Side 6. Balda Bay, the main one, was one of the largest structures ever created by man. Its enormous cylinder, with giant reflecting mirrors unfolding on three sides, slowly rotated in space and was home to over ten million people. He could already make out a string of lights around the colony much like those of an Earth city at night, and he knew he was looking at the colony's industrial zone; each light represented a module positioned around the port area that was used for the repair and the maintenance of ships and for the manufacture of goods. Since he had been raised in space, there was nothing particularly remarkable about the sight for him. His immediate concern was to find some way to dispose of his Core Fighter.

He walked several paces forward, hugging the shadow cast by one of the cargo containers lined up on the ship's deck. No one on the bridge could see him directly, but he also wanted to avoid anyone who still might be trying to snoop around his fighter.

Kusko Al put her helmet to his to initiate "skin talk," the low-tech form of communication preferred by Normal Suited people in space, which relied on transmitted voice vibrations. "Relax," she said, "there's no one else here."

Already sensing the same thing, he kicked off from the deck. In the weightless environment his body floated in a straight line away from the direction of the kick, toward his goal—the Core Fighter cockpit canopy. Reaching it, he opened an emergency hatch under its frame and yanked on a lever. The entire canopy popped open, and, just as he had feared, he saw that someone had removed the self-destruct explosive charge under the seat.

"Damn Zeon spies!" he cursed. Hastily, he opened a cover on the back of the attitude control computer module behind the seat. What looked like part of the computer was really a dummy box stuffed with a full complement of emergency explosives, ones that could be used for everything from flares to demolition. He proceeded to attach three units of explosives to the cables tethering the Core Fighter to the *Kasetta*'s deck and then started walking backward away from the fighter, unraveling a remote-control wire that terminated in a pull-ring safety switch.

And then it happened. A searchlight stabbed out at him. Although an alarm probably sounded inside the ship, out in space he couldn't hear it; instead, the wide-range receiver headset inside his Normal Suit helmet suddenly picked up the overlapping sounds of several voices barking, *"Who goes there? Don't move!"*

But it was too late. Amuro pulled the pin on the switch, and with a flash, the cables restraining the Core Fighter were blown apart, allowing it to drift slowly off into space. Kicking off the *Kasetta*'s deck, Amuro propelled his body toward the container where Kusko Al was hiding, and as soon as he reached cover, the fuselage of the Core Fighter suddenly swelled around the canopy, and then—*BOOM*—exploded. Fragments rained down on the deck of the *Kasetta*, showering several Normal Suited crewmen who had dashed out of the bridge area in panic.

When Amuro put his helmet next to Kusko's, he couldn't see her expression because of her sun visor, but he clearly heard her say, "Congratulations, Ensign . . ."

"Thanks. Now I don't have to worry so much."

"I'm happy for you. To tell you the truth, it was kind of exciting, but now comes the hard part."

"It was my capsule, and I had a right to do what I wanted with it . . ."

He felt her rest the left arm of her Normal Suit on his shoulder. He couldn't see her expression, but he sensed there was some underlying emotion accompanying it, one that he could only guess at.

"Tell me, why'd you help me?" he probed.

She answered, but not before laughing suggestively with the same tone he remembered hearing when he had first regained consciousness on the *Kasetta*. "Because you're cute," she said.

It was the last thing in the world he had expected to hear from her. She was clearly no Lala Sun. Brushing her arm off his shoulder, he stood up. Some of the *Kasetta* crew members were already running over.

"Please go in, Commander," said the round-faced secretary with the charming smile outside Krishia Zavi's office on *Abowaku*. Sha stood up, wearing a brand-new red uniform delivered only two hours earlier. Save for the fact that it was a little tight around his chest, it was quite acceptable. Given that it had been made by military tailors on a frontline base, it was nearly perfect.

"Hmph." He turned his head to see how the collar fit.

"It suits you very well, sir," the secretary remarked. She seemed unusually interested in the masked officer.

Just before Sha stepped inside Krishia's room, another officer exited. He hissed audibly as he passed by, saying, "So it's the masked young hotshot again," and Sha made a mental note to remember him. Through the open door he could see Krishia standing with her back to him, admiring her tropical fish. An aquarium one meter tall by three meters wide held several varieties, but a school of red swordtails dominated the whole tank, their scales flashing in the light.

"You must be tired, Commander," Krishia said as he entered.

He walked directly over to a chair in front of her desk. As always, he kept his mask on. Ostensibly it was to hide the disfiguring scar on his forehead and to protect his eyes, but he had an additional reason to wear it in front of her. He was afraid of being recognized because his foster father, Zinba Ral, had often told him that when he was an infant Gren, Dozzle, and Krishia Zavi used to play with him. Enough time had elapsed so that he was probably safe, but he knew that if he suddenly changed an old habit, it would only serve to arouse Krishia's suspicions.

"I read the combat report on the Elmeth," Krishia said. "Both you and many of the *Zanzibar* crew were lucky to get out of *Texas* alive."

"It's thanks to the people who built the colony, Excellency. It took quite a beating before it blew."

Krishia moved away from her aquarium. "It's too bad the Zeon patrol ships in the area weren't doing their duty," she grumbled, "or we could have rendezvoused earlier."

"It's too bad *Granada* didn't hold out a half day more," he replied. "If it had, I could have joined you in the fight."

Just before the *Texas* colony had exploded, he and several other *Zanzibar* crew members had escaped in launches and been picked up by a *Musai*-class Cosmo cruiser in the area on its way to participate in the defense of *Granada*. But on learning of the premature collapse of the base defenses, the cruiser had changed course. Making a broad detour around the moon, it had instead headed for Zeon's *Abowaku* space fortress, arriving only the night before.

Abowaku shared the same gravity-neutral Lagrange point as Side 3, which held the Zeon Archduchy. Constructed of two giant asteroids that had been transported from a remote belt, fused together, and fortified, it had the unique profile of an umbrella and was sometimes affectionately referred to as such. With *Solomon*—another man-made space fortress orbiting around Lagrange point 5—it formed Zeon's main line of defense. After fleeing *Granada*, Krishia had managed to reach *Abowaku*, obtain the use of part of it for herself and her surviving troops, and immediately begin reforming her forces.

"So you're another one who thinks we should have held out longer," Krishia said bitterly.

Sha was at a loss for words. He fully understood her frustration. If only *Abowaku* had been able to spare some of its forces, *Granada* might have been saved. The implication was clear. Gren, the supreme commander of the Zeon forces, had conspired with Dozzle and deliberately refrained from mobilizing to help her.

Rumor had it that Gren was secretly trying to isolate Krishia but that she had learned of his plans early and thus had deliberately fled *Granada* before it fell rather than defending it to the end. On seeing Krishia's reaction to his statement, Sha sensed that the rumor was indeed true, and if so, the Zavi ruling family was in even greater disarray than he had imagined. With luck, he thought, it might eventually collapse without his lifting a hand against it.

"It's the sort of thing that can't be helped, Excellency," he said, as if to console her.

It was such an obvious statement that Krishia laughed bitterly. "I just can't believe the way they treat us like such outsiders here at *Abowaku*," she said. "And it's not like Dozzle, but something's making him act awfully nervous, too.''

Abowaku was under the direct jurisdiction of Gren Zavi, not Krishia. Dozzle Zavi had come from *Solomon* to *Abowaku* to attend a reorganization meeting held the day before.

''And how is the plan to re-form your forces proceeding, Excellency?'' Sha asked.

''So-so. My *dear* brother, Gren, isn't easy on defeated commanders. But I'll show him. I've decided to form a New Type Corps.''

Sha suddenly felt uneasy. Krishia was acting impetuously. ''A New Type Corps?'' he asked.

''Gren may be supreme commander, but he has no idea of what's really happening here on the front lines. All he thinks about is what he's going to do *after* we win the war.''

''He's very confident, I'm sure,'' Sha said, empathizing. ''But do you really think the new strategy he's devised will work?''

Krishia looked both puzzled and shocked.

''I've heard it said,'' Sha continued, ''that he plans to lure the Federation Forces to a point directly between *Solomon* and *Abowaku* and destroy them in a single strike.''

''Are you talking about the System plan?'' Krishia's words suddenly had a hard edge to them.

''Er . . . yes.''

''Garma told you about that?'' Krishia's younger brother, Garma Zavi, Sha's former classmate at the Zeon Officer Academy, had recently been killed in action.

''I leave that to your imagination, Excellency. But I

don't think the supreme commander's goal is moving any closer to reality . . ."

"I quite agree. Nor does it seem likely that one single 'System' plan would be enough to end the war. We might succeed in annihilating most of the Federation Forces but still not be able to alter the course of history in favor of the Zavi family. I say that because I've heard that the Earth Federation Forces already have a New Type unit of their own. I'm of the opinion that the coming age may belong to New Types. Don't you agree, Commander?"

Sha was temporarily at a loss for an answer. Since directly confirming the existence of New Type individuals though Lala Sun, he was no longer cooperating with Krishia simply out of revenge and a desire to destroy the Zavi family. He was, in fact, in utter agreement with her comment about the next age belonging to New Types—making it come true had become his personal goal and ideology, but for different reasons. History clearly showed, he knew, that ordinary people were capable of resolving serious disputes only through war. New Types held out new possibilities.

He answered slowly: "A New Type age. . . . Yes, I think I can agree with that."

What he meant and what Krishia was thinking were totally different, but that was not his concern. It was currently in his interest to use Krishia and the Flanagan Agency she controlled. It was to his advantage to go along with her for the time being.

"I thought you would," she said. "That's why it's imperative for us to form a New Type Corps as soon as possible."

"I understand, Excellency, but I thought Ensign Lala Sun was the only true New Type we had available . . ."

"Don't worry. I didn't pour all that money into the Flanagan Agency for nothing. It just so happened that when you visited them, you only encountered the girl. In reality they have other New Type troops fully capable of operating in combat situations."

Krishia pressed a button on the intercom on her desk and asked her secretary to send in Commander Garcia Dowal of the Flanagan Agency. Then she stood up. "I understand you were on extremely good terms with Ensign Lala Sun . . ."

"Excellency?" Just like a woman, Sha thought. She *would* have to bring up just what he did not want to hear. "I was a little carried away by my youth, I suppose," he said in self-deprecation.

"Youthful ardor and kindness, Commander Sha. The very qualities which suit you least as a professional soldier."

He replied with a wry smile that was forced. He recalled Lala and how, from the very beginning, he had never really thought of her as a military person. How, through a series of coincidences, she had accidentally encountered the pilot of the Federation Mobile Suit, Amuro Rey, and how her mind had reached a mysterious harmony with his even in the middle of a duel to the death. Had she not been doomed, Sha knew her consciousness would have fused with that of the young MS pilot and reached even higher levels. The memory made him jealous; maybe, he thought, it was a good thing she had been killed. But he was also man enough to realize that if she truly represented the New Types people had long talked about, there might indeed be hope for mankind. Lala Sun and Amuro Rey had transcended normal love between men and women. Their fused awareness had expanded and strengthened into a type of universal wisdom. It held out the potential of a unification and purification of human desire and intelligence, all at the same time. *If only,* he thought, *it could happen to everyone . . .*

Commander Garcia Dowal was explaining to Krishia: ''Lieutenant Sharia Bull commands a fleet of ships that transport Helium 3 from Jupiter. When he returned to the fatherland two weeks ago, we had him investigated. He appears to be extremely promising.''

''But why,'' Sha asked, swirling the ice cubes in a glass of Scotch an aide had handed him, ''would a man of his caliber have been employed away from the front lines?''

''Perhaps it's some sort of prescience unique to New Types. Perhaps someone thought he could cause problems at the front.''

Garcia flipped through the file he held and began to read another page, but Sha stopped him.

''Don't you think it's a little odd? That the Flanagan Agency, er, excuse me, I mean you, would somehow manage to select someone like him out of all the others considered for investigation?''

''Sharia Bull? Why, he came to my group on the direct recommendation of Supreme Commander Gren Zavi . . .''

Sha was stunned. If, as he understood, Krishia thought that forming a New Type unit was exclusively her idea, here was Gren directly sending his own New Type candidate, and one who happened to be one of the most promising so far, as if to warn her. He didn't know what to say.

Garcia continued reading aloud from his file. ''And

then we have Junior Grade Lieutenant Kramer Karela. He's a former Zak pilot . . ."

When Garcia finished, Sha asked, "And is he at exactly the same level as Sharia Bull?"

Suddenly serious, Garcia answered, "Yes, the same as I mentioned earlier. But then there's also Junior Grade Lieutenant Kusko Al. She has such extraordinary abilities that the Flanagan Agency claims they had to put together special tests just for her. They even took her to Earth at great risk this week to see if any changes would occur in New Type brain wave patterns under the influence of normal gravity."

"To Africa, right? I heard about that. Tell us the result."

"We haven't received any information yet, but we should have a communication today."

"And where is this Kusko Al now?"

"She should be at Balda Bay, on Side 6 . . ."

Side 6 had an artificially created temperate climate. Some aspects of having four delineated seasons were inconvenient, but the Rank administration believed that people needed the stimulation. There were no annual rainy seasons or typhoons designed into the climate patterns, but heavy rains and snow were randomly scheduled every five years or so. It was a humble attempt on the part of humans to approximate the natural environment of their home planet.

The first day Amuro visited the Earth Federation consulate on Side 6, a Lieutenant List Hayashida offered him coffee and strawberry shortcake. One of twenty military attachés assigned to the consulate, List had been instructed to gather information, and he was more than willing to fill Amuro in on the details of the colony.

"We had a flood here once," List said. "I think it was in June the year before last. Twenty houses were swamped. It even became a political problem."

"Houses 'swamped'?" It was an utterly alien notion to Amuro.

"Sure. Even on Earth it never happens anymore. Rivers overflow their banks, and water inundates the houses."

"Really?"

"Really. But it doesn't affect me. I've got a great life here. All I have to do is check on the people who visit the Flanagan Agency. Every day I spend about four hours monitoring the agency entrance, compiling names and taking photographs of those who go in and out. Then I send the info to General Headquarters at Jaburo on Earth. That's it."

"What's the Flanagan Agency?"

"You don't know? I didn't realize you were *that* green, son. It's where the Zeon forces train their New Types. Surely you've heard of New Types?"

"But I thought Side 6 was neutral!" Amuro stabbed a strawberry with his fork and popped it into his mouth. "That's a violation of international law, isn't it?"

"Hah! Hah! Where have you been? Welcome to the real world. You can't be blamed for your ignorance, though, I suppose. They put you lads into the Force before you've even had the chance to chase a few skirts "

Picking up another piece of shortcake, Amuro weakly countered. "My superior officer used to say the same thing. But frankly, I don't think experience with the opposite sex has anything to do with it. Seems like an awfully jaded way to look at things."

"You know, I'll bet you'd drive some women out of their minds. You're the good-looking, innocent type of kid they'd just love to mother to death. But enough of that . . ."

List had apparently concluded that Amuro was something of an idiot. He took a gulp of coffee and stared out the consulate window at the colony's expanse of artificial hills and greenery. "The ways of the world," he continued. "Lemme tell ya something. When I leave the consulate, I put on a disguise. Sometimes I wear a fake beard. But someone from the Zeon side always tails me and watches when I photograph things from hotel windows or gather information at coffee shops. And when my four hours of work are over, the Zeon spy follows me back to the consulate. He works longer hours than I do. Understand? That's what being a spy is all about . . ."

"Seems a little devious."

"But that's the way the real world is. I've never had a gun battle with an enemy spy or anything exciting like that. That stuff only happens in the movies . . ."

Amuro nodded and sipped his coffee.

On arriving at Balda Bay, Amuro had at first been suspected of sabotaging the Core Fighter carried on the *Kasetta III*. He had expected a rough time with immigration and customs but then had been pleasantly surprised. As expected, Lt. List Hayashida, as a representative of the Federation consulate, had gone to bat for him. But so had Kusko Al. She, in fact, had turned out to be his biggest ally of all, speaking vigorously in his defense and even creating an alibi for him, testifying that he had been in her room when the Core Fighter had exploded. When the immigration officer had asked Amuro point-blank if her statement was true, he had of course replied in the affirmative. It was an outrageous lie, but her stubborn adherence to her story proved pivotal. It also enraged Isfahan, the aide on the *Kasetta.* *"She was sleeping with an officer from the Earth Federation!"* he exclaimed.

Lt. List Hayashida initially took the story at face value, but as befitted an intelligence officer, he eventually realized that Amuro was for all intents still a babe in the woods when it came to women. He had no idea of what had really happened between Amuro and Kusko Al. It was a mystery to him, but it was not his main concern. He had been specially commanded by General Revil, who had just occupied Zeon's *Granada* moon base, to take good care of the young ensign.

Amuro stared at the bluish tone of List's freshly shaved chin and decided to change the subject: "May I assume I can return to my unit soon?"

"Sure," the lieutenant muttered, pulling a photograph from his vest pocket and tossing it down on the table between them. "But take a look at this first . . ."

Amuro was stunned by what he saw. It showed Kusko Al, of all people, running up a flight of imitation stone steps. She seemed to be looking at the camera. Her full lips were formed in a smile.

"This isn't a one-time thing, pal. I wouldn't show it to you unless I knew what I was talking about. I saw her enter the agency three times, and just to make sure—since I've only been on the job here for a little over a month—I even checked my predecessor's records. Except for the last ten days, she's been visiting the Flanagan Agency almost daily for over six months. She's officially on the staff of the agency, but she's not a regular employee. She's a New Type."

"You must be kidding," a shocked Amuro whispered, picking up the photo and scrutinizing it. "Is this building the Flanagan Agency?"

"Hey, the photograph is yours. Use it for a reference."

"I . . . I didn't know . . ."

The lieutenant smiled weakly. Amuro looked up at him.

"So tell me," List said. "What's a Core Fighter?"

"It's an escape capsule for a Mobile Suit. It contains the entire cockpit."

"Of a GM Suit?"

"Yes."

"Something stinks here, Ensign . . ."

"What do you mean?"

"Listen, don't take it personally, but from my perspective you don't know zip about the ways of the world. There's something I don't understand going on here. I don't think you're leveling with me."

"Really?"

"Really."

"You probably want to say something about me being a New Type, but I'm not. I haven't had any special training at all."

"Well, how come I received a direct order from General Revil concerning you? I even heard your name from the immigration office. Ordinarily Federation military personnel are just checked for their identity and the unit they're attached to and then cleared. All I usually do is greet them at the port area. Don't you think it's a little odd Revil would personally order me to look out for you?''

''Maybe it's because my unit was annihilated on *Texas*.''

''Listen, don't play me for a fool, kid.'' List was getting visibly angry.

''No, it's true. I don't have any of the traits associated with New Types, and even if someone told me I was one, I wouldn't believe them. But . . .'' Amuro seemed suddenly to recall something. ''But what if I were?''

List stood up and informed Amuro that a Federation transport was scheduled to depart from Balda Bay the next morning at five. Then he announced, ''Kusko Al's a New Type. Her ID number's J6159. She'll leave the Flanagan Agency at six tonight and return to her quarters.''

Amuro smiled and said, ''Really? Thanks for the information.'' It dawned on him that he was being set up.

The Flanagan Agency had an official-sounding name, but it was housed in a nondescript building identified only by a worn, scarcely legible nameplate at the entrance. In front of the building there was a broad flight of ''stone'' stairs of over a dozen steps—the same stairs Amuro had seen in the photograph. The building was bordered by Himalayan cedar trees on a property facing a four-lane highway. It was a typical colony office building.

Amuro stopped an ele-car borrowed from the Federation consulate in front of the agency's parking lot. He knew List was probably tailing him, suspecting him of being a New Type, but he didn't even bother to turn around and check—List wasn't the type to blow his cover that easily. He gazed at the entrance to the building. It was long past normal closing time. Two or three people emerged and walked over to their cars in the lot without paying any attention to him. Then, suddenly, he saw a female figure exit, dressed in a knee-length skirt that fluttered as she walked. It triggered an odd reaction in him. On the *Kasetta III* he had seen Kusko Al only in slacks. Her chestnut hair bounced off her shoulders as she skipped down the stairs and came over.

"You wait long for me?" she asked.

"Less than thirty minutes," he answered, turning the key in the ignition. She sat in the seat next to him, and he sensed the power of her presence. It was a warm sensation, and he liked it. He had planned to check his rearview mirror before pulling out, but he was so distracted by the sight of her hair that he forgot. To his surprise, she said, "Don't even bother. Someone'll follow us, anyway." He stepped on the ele-car's accelerator and spun the car onto the highway in front of the agency.

"Sorry," he said.

"Sorry for what?"

"Sorry to lie in wait for you here like this."

"I saw you through the glass doors of the building entrance. What were you doing?"

"Lying in wait for you."

"I knew you'd come. I knew if you were at the consulate, you'd learn about this place. It's been three days, hasn't it? I knew you'd come. That's why I wore this skirt."

"Is this some sort of female intuition, or what?"

"Probably. I knew I'd never see you again if I suddenly had to go to Earth or relocate to the front lines. But I also knew if you were still on this colony, you'd come today.''

Kusko smiled happily as she said this, but Amuro sensed something else, something indicating that she was playing with him. Was it an illusion? He imagined her saying something like *''You really are kind of cute, aren't you.''* Tensing slightly, he smiled back and said, ''Mind if I ask you something else, Kusko?''

''Sure, go right ahead.''

''Are you using some special kind of psychology to figure out what I'm thinking?''

''I don't know anything about psychology, but we've been interested in each other since we first met. Hey, isn't that enough?''

She didn't call him ''baby,'' but Amuro sensed that she wanted to. She was only a little older than he was, but something made her sound like she was talking down to him. What was it? He wondered.

''No, I . . . I . . . uh . . . I don't think you understand,'' he stammered, quickly regretting that he had ever come to meet her.

''You really are kind of cute, aren't you?'' she said. And then she giggled.

Amuro stopped the ele-car. Kusko stopped giggling and stared at him. He stared back at her gray eyes, and in his peripheral vision he noted her beautiful skin and the lines of her body. ''Get out,'' he said.

''But. . . . I . . .'' Kusko was at a loss for words.

''Hey,'' Amuro said. ''If you think I'm such a kid, I'm not the man for you. Get out.''

''Listen, Amuro . . . I'm sorry. I didn't mean it at all. I was just happy to see you. I . . . I apologize if I offended you.''

"Well, don't be. I'm already taken. I already have a girlfriend—Fra Bow."

"I . . . I didn't realize," she stammered. "I'm really sorry."

And then she got out of the car.

"Sorry, Kusko," Amuro said as he punched the ele-car accelerator to the floor. He didn't understand why he was so angry. In reality, he had hoped to eat dinner with her and even go dancing. It all could have happened. And it would have been even better if they could have slept together. He knew all he had to do was turn the ele-car around.

Just when he was thinking he should pull over to the side of the road, two ele-cars passed him on the left. He straightened his steering wheel and drove straight ahead. In his rearview mirror he caught a glimpse of Kusko Al, standing, still waiting. Then he saw her turn around and start walking the other way. *I've got to go back for her,* he thought, knowing it was already too late.

Why had he mentioned Fra Bow's name to her? He couldn't understand it himself. Fra had been his neighbor on Side 7 and now was a refugee on Luna II. In spite of being younger than he was, she had always tried to mother him. She was more than his first love. She was almost like a sister. It *was* true she was waiting for him. He clearly remembered her telling him when they had parted. But he never should have blurted it out.

Why had he let Fra get in the way? If he really took his mission seriously, he probably should have had more contact with Kusko Al. He tried as hard as he could to calm his mind but found himself thinking things he had never thought of before. *Why did I act that way? Kusko Al was right . . . I was interested in her.*

The day was over on Balda Bay, and darkness was slowly falling on the entire colony. The tail lamps on his ele-car streaked through the night, and the street lights diffused into geometric patterns of light on either side as he passed them by. He cursed himself and stomped on the accelerator.

After the Federation Forces took over *Granada* and renamed it *FS*, for *First Step*, they were careful to deploy only enough forces to secure it as a beachhead—the former Zeon base was located at the southernmost tip of the Soviet mountain range on the far side of the moon and was thus directly exposed to Zeon's *Abowaku* space fortress. The Federation continued to keep its main forces on the other side of the moon—the side facing Earth—at a base code-named *LH*, for *Look Home*.

The *Trichigen*, a *Salamis*-class cruiser, slowly descended to the No. 6 deck on *LH*. It was a standard Earth Federation warship, and its basic shape conformed to that of the floating vessels that had once plied Earth's seas, but because it was designed for a weightless environment, it had subbridges protruding from both the port and starboard sides that could also be used as decks. Only for docking and coming alongside space piers did warships need a true "bottom."

Ensign Amuro Rey stood and watched from the bridge. After leaving Balda Bay on a civilian transport flying the Earth Federation flag, the *Trichigen* had come alongside specifically to take him on board, and for the duration of the flight he had been assigned a private room with a chief petty officer ten years his senior to care for him. It was VIP treatment normally only extended to senior officers, and it should have made him feel at home, but it didn't.

Like many combat-seasoned lower-ranking officers, Amuro had a rebellious streak that manifested itself in a regular hierarchy. He quickly became suspicious of his assigned aide, who followed him around like a shadow and liked to proclaim, "I'm under strict orders to take good care of you, sir!" The man's expression said the opposite, that if Amuro so much as tried to leave his prison he would knock his teeth in.

Amuro knew that Lt. List Hayashida, in accordance with his duty, had probably reported his meeting with Kusko Al in front of the Flanagan Agency. Given the fact that they had separated so soon after meeting, he also knew hardly anyone would believe he had only been trying to date her. No matter what he said, it would look like a furtive meeting of two people trying to exchange information. He could never explain it, but at the same time he hoped it would be overlooked. He had been picked up by the *Trichigen* and was now docking at *LH* because he had General Revil's special protection. The Federation military, he suspected, had far more pressing matters at hand than his encounter with Kusko Al.

On the bridge at least, the officers and crew treated him normally, but he nonetheless got the feeling that everyone from the ship's captain on down was keeping him at a distance. Perhaps they did not suspect him. Perhaps, since he would be with them only for the duration of the voyage and was unlikely to be assigned permanently to their ship, they had merely decided not to waste their energy in befriending him.

The *Trichigen* bridge communicated with the *LH* control tower one last time on docking procedure, and then a giant hatch opened over a huge shaft leading from the fortress's ground level to the underground decks of its port. The shaft extended over a kilometer deep into the moon's surface and held up to eight *Salamis*-type ships; descending all the way required passing through three different hatches. As a frontline base the area was poorly maintained and often had unsecured materials that easily floated free. As some scrap metal bounced off the bridge, someone yelled, "What's the matter with this place? Don't they have any gravity on the moon?"

If Kusko Al were really a New Type, it occurred to Amuro, he probably would never see her again. If they were both sent into combat, the odds that they would meet in the vast universe in which the war was being played out were surely less than one in a million. Why, he wondered, had he not spent more time talking with her the night before? Why had he suddenly become so angry? *I just hope I don't run into her the way I ran into Lala Sun,* he thought, regretting his impetuousness all the more.

Just when he was deciding it was all Kusko's fault, his eyes widened. The *LH* docking pier below seemed to rise up to meet them, and the *Trichigen* quickly decelerated to reach its assigned mooring spot. There were people in civilian clothes on the pier rushing about in preparation for the landing, and several military elecars were zipping in and among them.

Amuro instantly forgot about Kusko Al. "Hey,

look!'' he excitedly exclaimed to anyone in earshot. ''I'll be damned! My crew mates are there! There's Brite, my old skipper who's always flying off the handle! And Mirai, the ensign with the maternal instinct. And Kai . . . Kai Shiden. And look there . . . that's Hayato. They've all come to greet me! Hey, and there's Chief Petty Officer Mark! And Oscar! And that big heavyset man . . . That's Sleggar Row, the gunnery officer. And Ensign Ram Dowai, the engineer, with the big laugh. And wait a minute . . . that pretty blonde . . . that's Petty Officer Saila Mas!''

Two weeks had elapsed since the destruction of *Texas*, during which time he had assumed most of his friends had been killed. Now, seeing so many of them alive, he felt that an enormous burden had been lifted from his spirit. *So many had survived!* But one memory suddenly moved into his mind like a dark cloud on a sunny day. Ryu . . . Ryu wasn't there. Ryu, who had begun pilot training at the same time he had but had been destroyed in a Mobile Suit battle. If only Ryu were still alive . . .

When the *Trichigen* finally docked, the captain turned to Amuro and said, ''Congratulations on a job well done, Ensign. We look forward to hearing about your further success in the new 127th Autonomous Squadron.''

''The 127th?'' Amuro queried.

The skipper grinned and said, ''Well, it's just a rumor, but we hear it's an elite combat unit handpicked from the Federation Forces. If General Revil thought enough of you to have us give you VIP treatment, I'm sure you're among the pilots selected. I'm confident you'll perform superbly, Ensign.''

"Thanks, sir," he answered, resisting the impulse to tell him that he also knew the negative implications of any such assignment. He shook the man's hand, feeling terribly adult about the whole matter, and said, "Here's wishing the *Trichigen* good hunting, sir."

As soon as he disembarked onto the pier, Amuro heard a familiar voice cry out, "Way to go, Amuro . . . our star pilot. We knew you'd make it! Now tell us you're surprised to see *us* alive." It was his old comrade, Kai Shiden.

Amuro laughed. "Surprised? Hey, I'm amazed, especially to see *you*," he said. The crowd on the pier burst into laughter at the good-natured exchange, and he felt himself drawn into the mood of the moment. The informality of it all was perfect, and nothing could have pleased him more. He was reunited with his friends, with his old crew mates, and was filled with a profound sense of relief. It was almost like being reunited with a family.

"Good job, Ensign!" said Brite, his skipper. "A lot of cheers went up around here when we got word you'd made it to Side 6 alive. We've been waiting for you a long time."

Amuro looked around at everyone again and again, still not completely believing his eyes. And then he caught sight of the familiar blond young woman standing behind Petty Officer First Class Howd. He smiled briefly, and she smiled back. Her mouth seemed to form the words, "Welcome home, Amuro," but she was drowned out by the rest of the crowd.

"General Revil's waiting to see you," Brite announced, letting Amuro know he was not supposed to dawdle too long. There would be time to socialize later.

Mirai began hustling everyone toward four ele-cars

standing by. He noticed a new, confident air about her and wondered if it could be simply a result of surviving the ordeal on *Texas*. Saila jumped in Kai's ele-car behind Hayato. Ram Dowai, sitting next to Mirai in back of Brite's ele-car, yelled out for Amuro to join them, and he eagerly jumped in the front. It was hard to contain his enthusiasm. *"Yahoo! Step on it!"* he yelled gleefully. First Kai and then Brite accelerated forward, and the others followed.

The engines of the huge moored *Trichigen* shut down. When the boisterous former crew of the *Pegasus* left the giant domed underground port, the entire area was finally enveloped in silence.

Along the way Amuro's crew mates began to fill him in on what had transpired in his absence. "I'm sure you know," Brite said, "that the 13th Autonomous was completely successful in its feint maneuver. Despite losing our ship, we managed to lure several of Krishia's ships out into the open, and that helped the main force achieve a total victory in the Star One campaign. That goes without saying, of course; we wouldn't be here on this moon base if we hadn't won. All in all, things don't seem to be going well for the Zeon side."

"Think they're having some sort of internal power struggle, sir?"

"You could say that. Relations between the Zavi family members seem a little strained, to say the least."

"Really?"

"It's just a rumor, Amuro," Mirai added from behind him, "but people say there's a power struggle going on between Gren, Krishia, and Dozzle—the three surviving Zavi siblings."

"By the way, Mirai." Amuro suddenly turned and asked her teasingly, "Did you gain some weight?"

"Me?" She gasped and covered her cheeks with her hands. Her small round eyes practically popped out of her head. "Er . . . well, I guess I *have* put on a kilogram or two in the last ten days."

"I'll bet the military hasn't been giving you guys enough to do, that's what," Amuro said with a grin. "The Force is famous for poor communication horizontally in the ranks, right? They've probably forgotten all about you folks!"

"Sorry to disappoint you, Amuro, but things have been so busy here on *LH* recently, you'd probably wish you were off fighting instead."

"And that, kiddo," Brite injected with a mischievous grin, "is why everyone *really* wanted to come see you. They figured they could get out of a day's work."

Amuro was puzzled. Brite seemed to have matured by at least ten years. Was his extra confidence also simply that of a survivor?

"To tell you the truth," he said, "you all seem different to me somehow."

"Different?"

"Different. Maybe this is a weird thing to say, but everyone seems to be getting along so well now, almost like a family. I never sensed that before. Even Saila, the one everyone used to tease and call the 'bungler,' seems to be doing great."

"Maybe you're right," Mirai said. "Maybe it has something to do with having survived *Texas*. As for Saila, some of us did used to feel she was different and didn't really fit in. But it turns out she's the one who helped us all escape *Texas*. She's the one who showed us the way out of the colony before it exploded. It was like there was a mysterious voice leading her that none of the rest of us could hear."

Brite interjected, "You mean she might be sort of a New Type, right?"

"Well, maybe not as much as Amuro. Say, not to change the subject, but look at Kai and Hayato in the other ele-car, both vying for her attention."

"I'd say that's proof that she's finally been accepted," said Ram Dowai, seated next to Mirai.

"Amuro," Brite asked, "you're from the same Side as Saila, aren't you?"

"Yessir. Side 7."

When Amuro's ele-car finally arrived at the *LH* operations center, the other three vehicles were already waiting. Instead of getting out, their riders called out, "Go to it, Amuro!" "Good luck!" and "See you back at the *Pegasus*!" and then took off again. Saila smiled and waved, and after he had seen both Kai and Hayato jockeying for her favor, there was something reassuring about that.

Amuro and Brite got out of their ele-car, and Mirai took the wheel. "I'll see you both later," she said. "We're going to have a little celebration afterwards on the *Pegasus*—another excuse to take a break from work."

As they entered Operations, Amuro turned to Brite and asked, "Did I hear right, skipper? Did she say *Pegasus*?"

"She did. But it's really the *Pegasus II*. It turns out the Federation fleet had a second *White Base*–class warship, and we've all been reassigned to it. We're apparently going to form the core of the 127th Squadron."

Amuro fell silent for a second, realizing he was the only who had absolutely no idea what was going on. Then he asked, "We're shipping out again soon?"

"We sure are," Brite replied. "Time's apparently running out. The word is that Zeon's cooking up something a lot bigger than a little skirmish on the other side of the moon."

Inside Operations, General Revil took a puff on his cigar and let his eyes follow the trail of smoke. "I'm speaking to you, Ensign Amuro Rey, on the assumption that you may be a rare find—a true New Type. And I expect you to hold what I say in the strictest confidence."

"Yessir."

"Zeon forces have been lying low the last two weeks, but there's a reason. And it's not simply because they lost *Granada*. They're apparently developing a new secret weapon, one with awesome destructive power, and they're stalling for time."

Brite blurted out, "You mean they're going to put a New Type unit into action, sir?" When Revil ignored him, he stepped backward and looked down at the floor sheepishly.

"No, I'm talking about a weapon capable of directly hitting the moon from Zeon territory."

"A direct strike?" Amuro felt a chill run down his spine. That would be no mean feat. He had never heard of a beam weapon capable of inflicting direct damage from tens of thousands of kilometers away. In theory a long-range missile might work, but even if it emitted Minovski particles to confuse local defense radar systems, it would never be able to break through a defense perimeter of contact space mines. It was precisely because of those limitations that current military strategy still dictated the use of battleships for such attacks.

Revil laughed at the sound of Amuro's shocked voice. "I'm exaggerating, Ensign, I'm exaggerating." He stared at Brite as if to scold the overly young lieutenant for his earlier remark and then continued. "But not totally. Ever since the end of the twentieth century people have talked of a weapon that could instantly annihilate an entire fleet—talked of using an entire space colony to create a colossal laser cannon. It's exactly the sort of madness Zeon would seriously consider."

"Sir," Amuro said, "are you saying Zeon might use one of its sealed-cylinder colonies for that?"

"Exactly."

Brite interjected again, "But wouldn't they have to build a new colony cylinder specifically for the cannon?"

"Not necessarily. Don't forget, Gren Zavi's an absolute dictator. All he has to do is evacuate the residents of one of their existing cylinders and then reinforce its structure. It's probably not as difficult an engineering feat as it seems. We have information that they've already begun evacuating one."

Revil said it casually, but Amuro knew the scale of the operation would be mind-boggling. Even the most compact colonies were being built to house up to five million people. Large ones could hold ten to fifteen million. "I find it hard to believe anyone could carry out an operation of that size so fast, sir," he said, staring at the general.

"You'll find it easier to believe when you learn more about the political intrigues the human mind delights in. Don't forget that in the old days people used to take summer vacations in space—up to five hundred thousand people a month used to visit the *Texas* colony. We're only talking about Zeon mobilizing ten or twenty times that number. It's not impossible. And by the way, Ensign, to get back to the point your skipper made about Zeon forming a New Type fighting unit . . ."

"Sir?"

"That rumor may also be true. Which is why we've decided to form one of our own, with you at its core. That's what the 127th Autonomous Squadron's all about. We want you to be in the vanguard."

"*Me*, sir?"

"Surely you're not surprised. You must have been expecting it. After all, the Zeon Mobile armor you destroyed on *Texas*—the Elmeth—was clearly a weapon developed specifically for New Types. I know the general public might have been more impressed had you destroyed the Red Comet, but we military men know what a terribly important service you really performed."

"Er . . . thanks, I guess."

"I've made arrangements for your promotion, Ensign, but our staff seems a little bogged down with paperwork these days, so it might take a while for it to formally come through." Revil then picked up a letter of commission from his desk and handed it to Amuro, who stood up to receive it.

Amuro started to read from the paper, *"You are herein reassigned to the 127th Autonomous Squadron"*— when he was interrupted.

"That's correct," Revil said. "The performance of the *Pegasus* and its crew under the command of Brite Noa here has convinced me we should take a chance on *all* of you being potential New Types. There's no sense waiting for the desk jockeys at headquarters in

Jaburo to understand something like this. They've been working in their underground complex on Earth so long, they'd never believe that merely living in the vastness of space could alter human consciousness the way the New Type theory postulates."

The general ground out his cigar in an ashtray and stood up. "It's good to see you again, Ensign. I know you won't disappoint me."

"Er, th-thank you, sir. I'll do my best." He shook the general's hand and, despite the powerful grip, could tell the man was tired. It was no wonder.

"The general put his career on the line and fought tooth and nail with General Staff to get us assigned to the *Pegasus II*," Brite said as they left the office. "It seems like the Jaburo desk jockeys are an even bigger problem than Zeon."

Amuro pondered the meaning of Brite's words.

In the distance Commander Sha Aznable could see *Abowaku*, the odd umbrellalike shape of the floating fortress backlit by the rays of the sun. But he was more interested in what was going on inside the cockpit of his new model MS.

The accelerator pedal beneath his right foot was divided into three main stages, each of which could be precisely modulated. He floored it and noted that the entire MS cockpit, including his seat and the control panel, acted as a 360-degree shock absorber, canceling out much of the *g* force that would normally have borne down on him. He was delighted. The new model—a Rik Dom—would perform even better than his old Zak. It was larger in girth, and its armor was twice as strong, but it could turn on a dime. Moreover, the hand-held beam bazooka was directly linked to a highly efficient accelerator built into the arm, giving the MS the firepower of the main cannon on a *Musai*-class cruiser.

With this thing, he exulted, *I finally might be able to bag that white Federation Suit.*

Then a voice came over his receiver, so garbled by Minovski interference that it was nearly unintelligible: *"Here comes the target, Commander!"*

He barked verification into his mike, and his message was transmitted to the *Abowaku* operators by both radio and laser transmission. Several seconds later, when he was able to identify the target visually, he lined up the mono-eye sight of his MS with the bead on the beam bazooka barrel in its right hand. Then he pulled the trigger on the control stick, sending a laser-simulated beam streaking toward the target, and awaited a signal telling him if he had hit home. He had complete faith in his aim and used the intervening seconds to check the five Rik Dom Suits deployed on either side of him. They had not even sighted the target yet.

"Suits 2, 3, 4, 5, and 6!" he yelled. "Look above and to your right eighteen degrees! If this were real combat, you'd all have been pulverized! Scramble! You've gotta do better! Let's run this one more time."

How many times had they performed the same maneuver? He was beginning to lose faith in his men. In the last three or four moves executed they had always been too slow. None were new recruits. All were veterans, survivors from the beginning of the war, and all were skilled marksmen. Four had even bagged the ultimate prize—Federation battleships. Perhaps, he thought, the difference between himself and them was that he had more New Type potential. The futility of forming an effective, coordinated combat team with them grated on his nerves.

Another target appeared to streak out of the fiery sun, attacking the Rik Dom formation in a zigzag maneuver, and Sha pulled back to see how the others performed. He had to laugh at himself a little for even believing the notion that humans could improve dramatically overnight or suddenly become New Types. Perhaps, he thought with a tinge of bitterness, there had been only one real New Type: Lala Sun.

Then the garbled voice of the operator on *Abowaku* said, *"An Elmeth will be part of today's mock combat."*

"I thought that wasn't in the schedule today," Sha griped.

"Her Excellency, Krishia, specifically asked to see your team's performance against it, sir."

"Very well," he replied, "but it means we have to stay out here and practice for another five minutes." Before he could finish the sentence, he saw the flare of the Elmeth streak through the blackness. *I wonder if the thing is piloted by a human,* he thought. If so, no one had informed him.

"Formation G!" he yelled out to his men, initiating a defense tactic that had been devised to take on the white Federation MS—the Gundam—on the assumption that its pilot was a New Type. It involved deploying the six Rik Doms in an enveloping circle over an area five hundred kilometers in diameter. It was impossible to get a good look at the Elmeth itself at that distance, but the computers in their Suits would put them on a course estimated to bring them into contact, and the rest would be automatic. They would gradually close the noose around the enemy machine and try to sight it as soon as possible visually.

That was the theory, at least. Ten seconds later the Elmeth had slipped through their net and was closing in on one of the Rik Doms, attacking it without the aid of its remote-controlled auxiliary Bit units, instead using its twin particle cannon with devastating effect. When the fourth Rik Dom in the formation had been "destroyed," Sha knew what was happening.

"The Elmeth's not on remote. The pilot's real!" he yelled.

In the same instant he spotted the machine streaking above his own line of fire. He slammed his MS into an evasive maneuver and reflexively pulled the trigger on his beam bazooka. The shot was wasted. Then came another attack.

He aimed and thought he had the Elmeth in his sights, but it outmaneuvered him and dropped below his field of vision.

Sha yelled. He heard the simulated sound of something slamming into his Rik Dom and his fuselage creaking. Could he have been hit in the split second when his mind was diverted? The readout below his main monitor indicated that the left leg of his MS had been "shot" off. He put his machine into a retreat.

As he watched, in the next few seconds the Elmeth polished off the remaining two Rik Doms. The Elmeth's smooth skin swept upward at the rear, giving it the rather charming silhouette of a tricornered hat from the front, but its performance was far from charming. The Elmeth was deadlier than a humanoid-style Mobile Suit, and not because of its shape—which had little advantage over that of old-style space fighters—but because of its New Type pilot.

I bet they've found another woman to pilot the damn thing! Sha fumed. He sensed a unique presence emanating from the machine, something female yet unlike that of Lala Sun. Whatever it was, it possessed a defiant, abrasive quality. Could it be Kusko Al, the junior grade lieutenant candidate whom Garcia Dowal had mentioned? He feared a repeat of what had happened with Lala. He did not want to see another woman piloting the Elmeth.

The Elmeth floated right in front of his Rik Dom and then suddenly changed course. And sure enough, he caught a glimpse of a woman in a Normal Suit seated in an illuminated cockpit. He couldn't recognize her, but he knew the unusually large helmet of her Normal Suit was designed for a New Type. *Looks just like the one Lala wore,* he noted bitterly.

He barked out the order to re-form and the other Rik Doms fell into their conventional flight formation around him. He could see the rear of the Elmeth right in front of him.

Laugh at us if you want, he thought as he put his MS into second-level combat speed and soared past the Elmeth, his five comrades trying hard to keep up. For a second he imagined he heard the Elmeth pilot giggle. But in an instant a trail of light streaked across his main monitor and disappeared into a corner of *Abowaku*. It was the Elmeth.

"*Damn woman!*" he muttered. And then he heard—or thought he heard—a reply.

<I'm not a 'damn woman.' I have a name—Kusko Al.>

There was nothing audible. There were no words. A thought had simply slipped into Sha's mind.

"It's true we're putting a prototype into action, but we're not compromising on performance. We're talking about something fundamentally different from the new GM Suits. *Understand?*"

In the Mobile Suit development hangar on the Federation's *LH* moon base, Amuro listened to Professor Mosk Han lecture and realized that the man's authoritative, masculine demeanor was belied by a feminine tendency to overexcitability. Mosk was one of the most talented Mobile Suit engineers in the Federation, so Amuro tried to interpret his behavior in the best possible light and write off his outbursts as the product of an overly intellectual orientation to life.

"But Professor," he asked, "if you use a prototype MS design, I don't see how you'll be able to exploit the strengths of the magnetic coating."

"Hmph. You're trained not to think but just to sit in your cockpit and attack the enemy, so I guess it's *beyond* your comprehension, but the magnetic coating practically eliminates all the mechanical friction normally occurring in the MS power train."

"You mean it functions sort of like oil?"

"Oil? Did you say *oil*, lad?"

Amuro realized he had used the wrong word. Oil was an archaic term, and it appeared to have raised Mosk's hackles. "Well," he said, "I'm trying to understand, sir. I know that this prototype Gundam is the third model produced and that it was put through a pretty strenuous test period. But as the person who has to pilot the machine, I'd just like to make sure every potential problem is eliminated in advance."

"Well, that's clearly impossible. We've painted every single point of physical contact in the power train with magnetic coating. The positive and negative fields of the coating repel each other, thereby completely eliminating any mechanical friction. That's the theory. Understand? This is supposed to eliminate mechanical interference no matter what amount of force is applied.''

There was something Amuro wanted to say, but he held his tongue. He knew that eliminating mechanical friction would also eliminate the natural braking effect it could provide. And although the new MS body should be able to withstand almost any degree of stress—even if an engine ran into the red zone—he knew it still wouldn't have the speed or agility of movement he really wanted.

''But we still haven't solved the power problem, have we?'' he ventured.

''Of course not. What do you think I am, an engine specialist? But listen, since the resistance has dropped in the drive chain, the Gundam's actual overall mobility has increased between 120 and 130 percent. That's almost like installing a new engine that's twice as powerful.''

''Oh, I see.''

''Try it out. You'll be pleased. If we improved the MS performance beyond this point, your body wouldn't be able to keep up. You'd be constantly buffeted by enormous *g* forces, and in four or five minutes your insides'd be Jello. But I agree it's an area we've got to address eventually. We've got to find a way to create a cockpit that cancels out the *g* forces or else do something to your body so it can withstand them better.''

''Oh . . .''

''You're a clever lad. Keep me informed of the test results. And when you write out your reports, don't forget I'll be reading them, too.''

''Yessir.''

It was awfully difficult, Amuro realized, to judge people by first impressions. Those who seemed pleasant at first usually *were* good people. Professor Mosk had not been particularly pleasant, but the instant Amuro had changed his attitude to one of deference, he had become so friendly that it was uncanny. Perhaps, Amuro thought, it was a characteristic of technologists in his field.

While still pondering the Professor's personality, Amuro kicked off the hangar deck and sailed through the low-gravity air to the new Gundam's cockpit hatch. He was relieved that the Suit's basic humanoid design had not been tampered with and that, unlike the GM models, it still had two "eyes." If the machine was functionally going to reflect the pilot's will—*his* will—he wanted it to have some sort of expression. It need not be able to frown or raise its eyebrows like the crude pneumatic-powered Marilyn Monroe humanoid robots popular in shows in the last century. The two "eyes" were enough to create the emotive quality he wanted.

As always, the Gundam cockpit was encased in cold, steel-like material that felt like coffin walls. He shut the front hatch, whereupon the sound of the idling motor faded, leaving him enveloped in the Zenlike nothingness of total darkness. The instrument panel was inactive. Something about the air in the cockpit reminded him that maintenance people had been working on it a few minutes earlier, but it was freshly vacuumed and spotless. The pilot seat was as hard and uncomfortable as ever, but that was to be expected. Everything was more or less as he was accustomed to. The main control levers were on either side of him, and the foot pedals were in their appropriate locations. Even in pitch darkness he knew exactly where the twenty-eight switches of the control panel were. It was a relief. Switches, levers, pedals. All he had to do was stretch out his arms and legs, and everything was where it was supposed to be. *This should do fine,* he thought, *for the time being, at least.* He wasn't really sure where the thought "the time being" had come from or what he had really meant.

Peering around him, he knew it was not true, as some people said, that total darkness was frightening. He let his pupils dilate and still couldn't see a thing; in fact, he could hardly tell if his eyes were really open. He looked straight ahead and let himself relax. He listened to and counted his breaths. He became more aware of being alive and felt incredibly peaceful.

Then he heard, or sensed, a pinging noise. It was faint but it was soon accompanied by what felt like a tiny thread of light streaming out from the center of his brain into the darkness before him, through the hatch of the Gundam cockpit, through the surface of the moon above him, and into the vastness of the surrounding space. The light was sharply defined but had a warm, reassuring glow to it.

"Lala?"

Amuro shifted in his seat. He wanted to see where the light was headed, but it was already gone. It had not been a hallucination. He knew it had continued on into the black space before him. But he felt confused. *Lala Sun,* he thought again, and an indescribable aching sensation welled in his body, irritating and destroying his earlier tranquillity. A chill slowly crawled up his spine and spread out through his flesh until the ends of his limbs quivered.

Lala Sun . . . is it Lala Sun? Something in his mind nearly screamed the thought. He felt even more annoyed. *What are you trying to tell me? Lala . . . or whoever you are. What is it?*

He knew he had to do something. He put his hand on one of the Gundam's control levers and squeezed it. Then he turned the key in the ignition and through the floor of the cockpit felt the engine groan before fully igniting. When the instrument panel sprang to life, its lights nearly blinded him with their sudden brightness and instantly banished the entire black universe before him. They had two stages of intensity, and when they reached the second, he knew the main engine had fired. With a *VROOM*, the Gundam revealed its inner power.

Then he knew part of the source of his frustration. The machine enveloping him was a weapon. *Are New Types,* he wondered, *merely an extension of a weapon? Just another tool of destruction? Is that what Lala Sun was? Is that what the Red Comet is? Is that all I am?* He was flesh and blood. Not a machine. He wanted desperately to refute such a repulsive idea and assert a higher purpose in life for himself, but a swirling undercurrent of self-doubt undermined his ability to do so.

New Types are humans. He pushed the right-hand control lever forward, and the Gundam's right arm rose with a burst of energy, far faster than the old model and with enough force to make the entire MS fuselage recoil. But with that movement Amuro's own reflexes also came alive, and his limbs began moving the other controls in the small cockpit, working rapidly to keep the Gundam properly balanced.

A team of mechamen who had just finished a job in another corner of the hangar turned and stared at the Gundam. It was standing with its back still attached to a maintenance fixture, but its limbs began slicing through the air. One man yelled to his comrades, "Hey, get a load of that, will ya? That shows what magnetic coating can do!"

The new Gundam was infinitely more maneuverable than either the original model or the mass-produced GM Suits currently in use, and its next maneuver was truly astonishing. Its left arm slowly rose in the air, paused for a few seconds, and then slammed downward, but the body of the machine scarcely twitched, despite having moved off the supporting fixture. By slightly shifting the Suit's hips, Amuro had canceled the weight of the mass in its arm perfectly. To the cheers of the mechamen, he then began moving the Gundam with such speed and grace that it looked more like a human boxer than an inorganic machine. In theory, it should not even have been possible.

An order then issued from the control room. *"Number 6 hatches will open shortly. All personnel in hangar area must move to the air lock!"*

The mechamen in the maintenance area ran for cover to the air lock room and clustered around its one-meter-square blastproof window, transfixed. The new Gundam began striding forth.

After passing through the double-layered hangar hatches, Amuro entered the vacuum area of the moon base. On the Gundam's surrounding displays he saw a sliver of Earth shining in the distance, surrounded by stars blazing in the heavens. He announced into his mike: "Ensign Amuro Rey in G3, ready for launch. Now commencing practice flight!"

The base flight control officer replied, stating what they both already knew: *"Take it away, Ensign. Re-*

member, you're out there to get used to the Suit's flight characteristics.''

Amuro double-checked his radar and laser-sensors. Neither would be much good with the high Minovski concentration in the area, but the lasers could at least act as a Friend or Foe (FOF) ID signal, and there was something reassuring about having radar even if it didn't work. He looked up at the heavens through his main display, double-checking the area in space from which his computer was registering information. Somewhere out there he knew a space beacon would delineate the practice area for him.

''Blast off!''

He said it half to himself, half as a formality to inform the flight officer. He fired the main rockets in the Gundam's backpack, and to his astonishment the Suit soared nearly ten thousand meters in seconds. The new model was far faster than he had expected. The laser accelerator in its nuclear fusion engine had been improved, theoretically yielding only twenty to thirty percent more power, but when combined with the new magnetic coating on the power train, the resulting synergy seemed to create a nearly 200 percent increase in both power and speed.

Yet he was still bothered by one thought: *If only the armor had been reinforced, too.* There was something disturbing about improving the machine's performance without improving his own personal protection. He understood the logic behind the changes made, but *he* was the pilot and the one whose life was on the line. Perhaps he was asking too much, but he was human. Perhaps, he imagined, it was even something Lala had tried to warn him about earlier.

He was sure of one thing—the issue of New Types

and their future transcended his personal safety. He knew the leap in consciousness, the sense of prescience he had experienced with Lala Sun, was not limited to them alone. Their special communion had heightened their five senses and expanded the fundamental communication of which *all* humans were capable. And in the end it had generated a mysterious, compound universal wisdom. It was an experience, he was convinced, that led beyond personal oblivion.

But if Amuro was a potential New Type, he was also an ensign in the Federation Forces, a military pilot. And military pilots were not supposed to ponder the future of mankind. They were supposed to kill and survive to kill again. To stay alive and develop as a true New Type he would first have to conquer the vast obstacle unfolding before him, the battlefield of outer space. It seemed like a cruel fate, but whether military pilot or New Type, his fundamental emotional makeup was the same, and he knew that he would just have to wait and see what happened.

The new Gundam Mobile Suit was painted a deep gray and therefore was harder to detect visually in space, and it had been designed to be even more invisible to radar. To make certain accidents did not happen during training flights, it had running lights for identification on its shoulders and toes. To Amuro's left and right the lights streaked through the space among the stars.

On the bridge of the *Pegasus II*, Chief Petty Officer Mark Kran suddenly sighted a unique laser oscillation on the computer-generated model displayed on the ceiling and called out, *"It's the new Gundam!"* The computer system was even less reliable than radar, but at it was at least capable of detecting and encoding laser signals.

"Three degrees to port! Elevation thirty-six degrees! Distance 180 kilometers!" barked Petty Officer Oscar Dublin, perched opposite Mark on the bridge's boom crane.

Brite scrambled down from the captain's seat at the base of the crane arm, ordering, "Saila! Open a radio link! The Gundam's coming in for a test landing on Deck 1."

"Gundam! G3!" Saila announced, her eyes intent on the communications panel in front of her. *"This is* Pegasus II. *Can you read us? Over."* She sounded so professional, it was hard to believe that she had once been a fresh recruit derisively referred to as the bungler.

Amuro's voice burbled up through the static. *"This is G3. I read you! My instruments confirm the* Pegasus II . . ." In a heavy concentration of Minovski particles, it took a highly trained communications operator to understand what he was saying.

"Pegasus *to Gundam,"* Saila replied. *"We have opened the hatch on Deck 1 for you. You are cleared for landing!"*

"Understood! Landing at third combat speed. Incoming!"

Brite turned to Mirai, standing with her hands on the helm. She switched it to automatic and ran to the bridge window to see the Gundam.

"He came into view awfully fast, didn't he," she said.

"That's Amuro for you," Brite replied.

"I'll say. The ace of the 127th."

* * *

Pegasus II, the second *White Base*–class Cosmo cruiser in the Federation arsenal, was designed as an assault landing ship, but it actually resembled a giant winged horse. In the vacuum of space the wings performed no aerodynamic function but acted as heat dissipation panels and held the ship's solar energy cells and many of its vernier jets. They were so huge that on Earth they would have made the ship appear capable of leaping through the stratosphere. The main bridge of the craft, protruding forward near the prow, looked like the head of a horse, hence the name of the first ship of this class: *Pegasus*. The second ship had been christened with the same name because the original crew had been transferred to it and because General Revil believed in "luck."

As the officers on the bridge marveled, the Gundam approached the *Pegasus II* and logged the correct coordinates for landing on Deck 1 in the ship's right front "leg."

The upper and lower hatch doors of Deck 1 opened, exposing the landing floor and its approach lights. The Gundam moved straight toward them, a line of horizontal green lights on either side of the deck blinking in confirmation of its course. Simultaneously, indicators showing horizontal status, attitude, and speed relative to the ship blinked in synch on Amuro's console—laser sensors were accurate at distances under two thousand meters, even with a heavy Minovski concentration. The hatch quickly looming into view was huge, but the landing site still wasn't an easy target. The Gundam sailed toward the center of it, streaking by painted white guidelines. Then, with a *whoosh*, retrorockets fired, its knees bent to absorb the shock, and both legs hit the ground simultaneously. Amuro had made a perfect single-point landing.

"Congratulations, Ensign Amuro!" Kai Shiden's voice echoed from the upper left three-inch minimonitor in Amuro's cockpit. *"It looked beautiful!"*

Amuro grinned bashfully at the image on the screen. While releasing his seat belt, he replied, "I used to be able to fly by the seat of my pants, but I think I forgot how. I broke out in a cold sweat a couple of times back there!"

On the next monitor over, the face of the flight deck supervisor appeared, yelling, *"G3! Stand by for thirty seconds. Do not open your cockpit hatch until air intake is completed on Deck 1!"* It belonged to a young recruit Amuro had never seen before, who immediately introduced himself. *"Petty Officer First Class Callahan Slay, sir! At your service, sir!"* He seemed so zealous, Amuro wondered if he would be able to stay calm in times of crisis.

"Glad to be working with you, Callahan. Twenty seconds have already elapsed!"

"Twenty seconds . . . yes, sir! Go ahead and open the hatch, sir!"

Amuro pulled a lever and opened the cockpit hatch. It shared space with his main display, which meant that to exit he had to use a footrest built into the far right side of the console panel and then ease his torso out. A ramp from the right wall of the flight deck extended out to his cockpit.

"Well, how was it?" It was Lieutenant Seki, the ship's engineer, whom Amuro had known ever since his days on Luna II.

"No problem, sir! The magnetic coating seems to work perfectly."

"Well, I'll still give it a once-over to check for anything unusual. You know how it is . . . I've got to compensate for those scientists and the top brass. They always tend to rush these things."

"You think there might be a problem with the coating, sir?"

"If there is, it's a relative problem. The structural materials used in the Gundam design aren't going to get any stronger. In some ways it's safer if you can't move the thing too fast."

"Sounds to me, sir, that you're saying we need to compromise on speed for safety's sake."

"Exactly. But we're talking about a combat Suit here, so combat performance gets priority. The brass apparently assume anyone operating this thing has the skills of a test pilot."

"Ha, ha." Amuro laughed despite himself. There was more than a little irony in Seki's words. After all, the *Pegasus II* and its entire crew were part of a grand experiment. They were all in a sense test pilots.

"Basically, Ensign, I want to keep you alive as long as possible."

"The sentiment's shared, sir," Amuro replied, removing his helmet and starting to walk down the ramp to the flight deck.

Then he heard a "Yo" and saw a smiling face in a lemon-yellow pilot's suit. It was Kai Shiden.

"Say, Kai," he asked, pointing at a new red MS to the rear of Deck 1, "is that Gun Cannon over there the one you're piloting?" Gun Cannons, like the Gundam, were of humanoid design and had two arms capable of holding a beam rifle, but they were not as well suited for close-quarter combat as the Gundam or the GM models were. Instead, they had two 28-

centimeter cannons built into their shoulders and were used primarily for long-range support.

"Yeah," Kai answered without enthusiasm. "That's the C108. It'll do the job, maybe."

Kai didn't have the type of positive personality Amuro normally admired, but the two of them had begun their pilot training together, had survived combat together, and now were linked by a bond different from friendship but just as real.

"Everyone's waiting, partner," Kai said.

Since being reunited with his comrades on the *LH* docking pier, Amuro had spent two days alone working with Mosk Han, readying the new Gundam. Now he would finally, hopefully, be able to spend a little time relaxing with them on the ship. Just thinking about it made him feel flush with anticipation, but there was still an enormous amount of work to do. The *Pegasus II* carried five Mobile Suits including the Gundam, and several hours would be required to train the Suit pilots to work as a team, in formation. Amuro's first assignment, therefore, was to lead a special training session on the ship's bridge.

The moment he stepped into the room, he was warmly welcomed. Lt. (jg) Brite, in the captain's seat, saluted and barked, "Congratulations, Ensign!"

"Well, how was the flight?" Mirai asked.

"You looked great out there, Amuro. Well done," Hayato added.

Amuro first noticed the new faces among the group, including Ensigns Sarkus McGovern and Kria Maja, both new MS pilots. But he also saw some old ones. Mark Kran and Oscar Dublin grinned at him from their operator seats on the bridge boom crane, and when

Saila Mas turned around and smiled at him, he nearly choked.

With her blond hair and nearly perfect posture, she looked more beautiful than he remembered. Perhaps, he suddenly thought, she really was the woman of his dreams. He felt a little confused. Before taking off in the new Gundam from the *LH* moon base, while sitting in the pitch blackness of his new cockpit, he had experienced a sort of intuitive communion with the memory of Lala Sun. But there had been something missing with Lala. And here it was. For the first time since parting with Kusko Al, he felt physical desire.

"Congratulations, Ensign," Saila said. Her clear voice sounded like music to his ears.

I never realized how much I wanted her . . .

Surprised at himself, Amuro decided to invite her to join him that night.

CHAPTER 12
PEOPLE

"For the life of me, I can't understand why Gren would call me back to the fatherland on the eve of our showdown with the Federation."

In the vast hall of the Zeon War Council, Vice Admiral Dozzle Zavi deliberately blurted out the words loud enough so that his father, Archduke Degin, seated on his throne, could easily hear them. Dozzle's elder brother, Gren, the supreme commander chairing the council, did not react at all and merely continued to lord it over those in attendance. He was flanked by both Dozzle and his sister, Rear Admiral Krishia, and a bevy of ranking Zeon officers under Zavi family control.

Technically a civilian government ruled Zeon, but even the layout of the room reflected a bargain struck between image and reality. Prime Minister Darshia Baharo, along with several ministers under his influence, was one of the few civilians to rise to power through the ranks of the bureaucracy and was thus supposed to have been given the seat of honor near Archduke Degin. But since the Zavi family depended on the military, he was seated the farthest away. One-third of his cabinet ministers were controlled by the Zavi family. Degin, nominally an observer, had already been reduced to a puppet. True power lay in the hands of Supreme Commander Gren Zavi.

An occasional reluctance to conform had created a suspicion in some quarters that Prime Minister Darshia harbored a desire to depose Supreme Commander Gren and restore Degin to power. Gren was fully aware of the rumor yet was prepared to tolerate it. He was accustomed to scheming minds and knew that intrigues were a normal part of human nature; as long as they were not an overt threat, he knew that there was no use trying to suppress them completely, that to do so would only be counterproductive. As long as Darshia was restrained, therefore, he would not take action against the man. All he had to do, he believed, was tighten the reigns of control and make him subtly aware of the futility of his scheming. That was the type of man Gren was. He would let his brother Dozzle raise as much fuss as he wanted. As long as there was no major change in the overall picture, he knew his position was secure. He could trust his sister Krishia to keep the rest of the situation under control.

"Vice Admiral Dozzle," Krishia said, replying to her brother's earlier comment, "if, as we suspect, the Federation Forces have detected what we are up to, then I respectfully submit that there is only one issue that must be urgently addressed today, and that is the state of progress on our System project. We must keep our perspective!"

Gren noted that, as he had hoped, Krishia was working to keep Dozzle in line.

Krishia glanced at Gren after her statement and then turned to Prime Minister Darshia. "We need you to give us an overview of the System project as proposed by the supreme commander."

Darshia thereupon launched into a prepared presentation. It was the first time most of the officials present had heard of the plan, but the principle behind it was elegantly simple. Zeon's older design of colonies consisted of sealed cylinders six kilometers in diameter by thirty kilometers in length. The inner walls of one of them would be coated with aluminum. Solar energy would be stored and concentrated in a powerful electromagnetic field inside and then released by suddenly opening one end of the cylinder. It entailed a massive construction project and would thus take time, but if all went as planned, the result would be a weapon of unprecedented destructive power, a giant laser cannon six kilometers in diameter. If it were properly aimed, an entire battle group, perhaps even half the Federation Forces, could be instantly annihilated. For the Zeon Archduchy, whose forces were from the beginning limited and were now nearing the point of exhaustion, the System, as the project was code-named, was an extremely attractive strategy.

"The cabinet," Darshia announced, "wishes to keep Zeon's civilian casualties to a minimum, and to do this we must bring the war to its earliest possible conclusion. We therefore have resolved to endorse the System project."

The prime minister's announcement was important, as without a national consensus the project could never be completed. The System required not only a massive budget but also the evacuation of over three million people from an older existing colony and the cooperation of a wide variety of industries.

"Hmph," Dozzle sniffed. "What do we need a cabinet resolution for?"

"Hold your tongue, brother," Krishia retorted, again restraining Dozzle just as Gren had hoped.

Darshia raised his voice another notch and continued, "Accordingly, given the nature of this measure, we wish to propose that it be seriously discussed by all parties in attendance today and then, in order to obtain the final authorization of His Excellency the Archduke Degin, that it be submitted for formal approval."

Two or three questions then followed, all of which revolved around the prospects of total victory. There was no need to debate anything else. Unbeknown to most civilians present, the project was already well under way, and the evacuation of the No. 3 Zeon colony cylinder, *Mahar*, was proceeding under the supervision of a high-ranking Zeon officer.

The council fell silent for several minutes. All present sensed the tightening web of Gren's total control. But distracted by all the attention to a single grandiose strategy or by the fate of this or that Zeon warship, few truly realized that the Zeon nation had begun to move in a direction of its own. It was, needless to say, a direction totally different from what they suspected.

Prime Minister Darshia took the cabinet's written proposal, placed it in a black leather file with the Zeon Archduchy seal, and walked toward Degin. No one in the hall spoke. Gren kept staring at the long tabletop in front on him, and his face took on an ashen hue. Darshia ascended the three steps in front of Degin's throne, placed the file on a stand next to it, and stiffly slid it toward the archduke. And then he heard words that made him doubt his own ears.

"My eldest son is a blot on my honor," Degin whispered. "Do with him as you please."

The archduke had never uttered such a thing before, even behind closed doors. *Perhaps he's becoming senile*, Darshia thought for a second. He stared at Degin's spectacles, trying to fathom the expression in the eyes behind them, but the man already reached out for a pen to sign the document and his face was turned away. Darshia hoped the words he had heard were a figment of his imagination. He was a civilian with precious few connections in the military elite. His real role in the government was to present a civilian face to the Zeon people. Like Degin, he was really only a puppet, and what could a conspiracy between two puppets possibly accomplish?

Degin put down his pen, smiled, and whispered words unrelated to his expression. "It's Krishia, isn't it?"

What did he mean? Darshia thought. Was he trying to say that he should use Krishia to crush Gren? As far as Darshia was concerned, Krishia was just as formidable a threat as Gren.

"Thank you, Your Excellency," he nonetheless replied, returning Degin's smile. Then he turned around and walked over toward Gren. When viewed from behind in his military uniform, Gren's neck looked as thick as a log, invulnerable to even the blade of a beam saber. Darshia opened the file and showed Gren his father's signature.

"Well done, Darshia," Gren said. He normally looked at people with a cold, piercing expression, but his mouth was now formed into a thin smile.

"Thank you, sir," Darshia answered. Then he turned to either side, showed the same file to Dozzle and Krishia, and after receiving their acknowledgment returned to his own seat, the lowest in the hierarchy.

Then Gren addressed the council:

"One hour from now we shall hold a comprehensive strategy meeting at the Unified General Headquarters. Let me humbly express my appreciation for the time and wise counsel you have all invested in this issue. Like us, the Federation Forces are nearing exhaustion. But a new element has been introduced into the balance of power. Now that the System plan has been authorized, we have gained the equivalent strength of between five and ten new divisions! I am proud to say, frankly, that our decision has altered the odds of victory in our favor. It is an accomplishment that every citizen of Zeon should take pride in, for the System project is a crystallization of all our labor and sweat. The System strategy will henceforth be the centerpiece of our operations. I ask now that each and every one of you take this fact fully to heart, and exert your utmost to destroy the Federation Forces as soon as possible and thus gain honor for the Zeon Archduchy. May you and your families prosper. Death to our enemies!"

In the midst of Gren's speech, Degin Zavi stood up and left.

By the time the *Pegasus II* and its five Mobile Suits had finished practicing their combat formation flight and returned to the *LH* moon base, it was already past seven o'clock mean time. Several *Salamis*-class cruisers were moored in the base docking bay, and preparations for the upcoming mission were proceeding at a feverish pitch.

Before leaving the bridge Amuro loosened his pilot's suit and turned to Brite in the captain's seat. "When do we ship out next, skipper?" he asked.

"How the hell should I know? You think they'd tell me? All I know is we have to perform all preflight maintenance within twenty-eight hours."

"And we take off right after that?"

"I doubt it. We're talking about image and reality here. But there is a possibility we'll have to leave even earlier, so you'd better get as much sleep as you can tonight. My gut feeling is that we'll be here another two nights, but who knows?"

"Understood, sir. Do you think my stuff has been delivered to officer's quarters on base?"

"Your stuff?"

"Just one duffel bag, that's all."

"Probably."

"A duffel bag" was military slang for a waterproof denim sack that held a single standard-issue military uniform. It was an anachronistic term in the space age but still popular, a holdover from the naval traditions of a bygone era.

Turning to Petty Officer Saila Mas, Brite said, "He doesn't seem to know anything about this place. Show him to his quarters."

"Yessir," she replied. She was engrossed in her work at the communications console, and she quickly told him, "Give me two or three minutes, okay?"

Amuro watched Brite monitor the preflight checks on the bridge displays and bark his orders throughout the new ship. He couldn't help thinking how much things had changed and how fast. The bridge was bustling with activity and alive with a new energy. Was it because many of the crew members were potential New Types? There was no way of knowing for certain, but there *was* a palpably different, though intangible, aura about them. It was unlike the emotive communion he had sensed with Lala Sun, and for a moment he wondered if the difference was simply because he was not properly attuned to them, but he soon decided otherwise. There was something clear, soft, even reassuring in the atmosphere. It was a peaceful feeling, almost like home. There was no point dwelling on the reasons. Had it not been wartime, with all its attendant tensions, he would have abandoned himself to the sensation and been lulled into a deep and restful sleep.

"Sorry to keep you waiting."

At the sound of the overly polite voice, Amuro turned around to see Saila. She was carrying a thick file, which reminded him of the studious young woman he had first encountered on Side 7's Zeravi library. But she seemed tired. It was odd, because she had been so energetic when working earlier. And standing close to her, he sensed more than fatigue, something closer to melancholy, for lack of a better term. For some reason he was suddenly aware of the fact that she was of the opposite sex. He wondered what was troubling her and what to do but decided not to dwell on it. Her mood was probably just a normal part of her emotional makeup.

"This way." She turned away from him and walked toward one of the two hatches in the rear of the bridge. He followed, watching. She was a year or two older than he was but a tad shorter. As usual, he admired her pretty blond hair. When they reached the elevator that would lead them out to the docking bay, he asked, "Well, have you finally gotten used to life on ship?"

"Why, yes, thank you," she replied. "At least I don't

get in everyone's way anymore. And by the way, I'm glad you made it back okay, Ensign."

"Whoa, please, let's cut out the rank. You'll embarrass me."

Seeing his obvious confusion, she said, "Well, I'm a petty officer second class; you're an ensign. This is the military, isn't it?"

"Well, yes . . . but dammit . . . Don't be too hard on me, Saila."

"Just between the two of us, then, what should I call you, Ensign?"

"Er . . . um . . ." Unable to answer properly, he began to grind his teeth. It was weird. Here he was, a seasoned combat veteran. Somehow he had assumed that would help him relate to her on a more equal, adult basis, but so much for that idea. He was stammering away, another naive delusion shattered. He fell silent.

Twenty seconds later the elevator stopped at the ship's upper deck, and the instant the door opened they were enveloped in a cacophony of sound. *They oughta let the air out of the hangars when they do preflight maintenance and supply operations,* Amuro thought reflexively.

The upper deck was at the base of the ship's bridge, and from it one could look out the open hatches of the starboard and port leglike extremities. The hangars of the *LH* docking bay were on two staggered levels, and on the lower one a transport ship that had moored was busy unloading ammunition and weaponry. On the upper level work crews Amuro had never seen before were engaged in a flurry of activity and were clearly the source of most of the noise. They were already welding parts of the *Pegasus II* deck and even stripping off parts of its armor.

Amuro tried to cross over to the mooring pier but tripped on a ladder and grumbled despite himself at an officer in front of him holding a transceiver. "What the hell's going on?"

"What's the matter? The repairs bother you?"

The officer turned around and Amuro had to stifle a gasp. It was Matilda Ajan, the pretty junior grade lieutenant from the 28th Supply Corps, whom he had met once before on Luna II.

"Ensign!" she said, as surprised as he was.

As when they had first met, he noted her auburn hair. It was a shame she kept it so short.

"I . . . I'm sorry . . . I was out of line," he mumbled.

"Never mind, Ensign . . . Ensign Amuro Rey, isn't it? I remember you. Lieutenant Woody Malden's in charge of the repairs, and you can trust him one hundred percent. He says the *Pegasus* needs a more consistent thickness of armor plating."

"Lieutenant Woody Malden?"

"An officer from the armory." She pointed with her chin in the direction of an officer engineer with a powerful physique, who turned around as if on cue.

Amuro silently mouthed the name "Woody" but couldn't think of anything to say. The timing between Matilda and Woody could have been accidental, but he was sure it was not. The officer had responded in a special way to her. He was a handsome man with heavy eyebrows and full lips, twinkling eyes, and an active demeanor, exactly the type he suspected Matilda would go for. And he was in a unit with which she would naturally have a lot of contact.

"You say something, Matilda?" Woody asked, walking over toward them. He seemed to have absolutely no trouble handling moon gravity. *He looks and acts like a real combat veteran,* Amuro thought.

"No . . . no, sir," Matilda replied. "This is Ensign Amuro Rey. He was just asking what you're doing."

Amuro heard a slight tremble in Matilda's voice and turned away from the pair in embarrassment.

"Some problem?" Woody asked.

"No, *sir*!" Amuro fired back. "Just an opinion stated without knowing the facts. I'm sure the *Pegasus* is in good hands." He saluted and jumped off the ladder toward the pier itself.

"Amuro!" Saila called out after him as he sailed through the low-gravity air.

When the concrete surface of the pier filled his vision, Amuro flexed his knees and landed. To his surprise, Saila landed beside him only seconds later.

"Amuro! What are you doing?" she cried, regretting her choice of words before she had completed the sentence. She felt flustered herself.

He sensed her emotion, but he was not ready to think about its implications. He was still preoccupied with Matilda Ajan and the sudden realization that she was in love with someone. He had no idea why it bothered him. He didn't have a crush on her or anything like that, he told himself, although he knew his reaction spoke otherwise. He was feeling self-critical, and it occurred to him that he was simply too immature and inexperienced around women. Just having a woman like Saila or Matilda stand in front of him was enough to overload his brain and paralyze him. He could never compare himself favorably with Woody, for example. He knew that if Matilda so much as tossed her auburn hair and moved toward Woody, the officer would grab her right away. It made him feel all the more humiliated.

"Amuro!" Saila said, grabbing his left arm.

"What?" he said, noticing her blond hair again. She was so different from Matilda.

"That building over there . . . that's the quarters you've been assigned to," she said with an official tone. Most men would have detected a tinge of jealousy in her words, but Amuro was oblivious to it.

She helped him check into the facility, where he was assigned his private quarters. As an ensign, he was on a different floor than Saila, who was housed with the junior officers. Before stepping into the elevator to go to his room, he turned to her and asked, "Will you join me for dinner tonight?"

"But Amuro, you're probably busy and tired, right?"

"Uh . . . no . . . heck . . . Besides, I don't get the chance to eat with you very often. I'd be honored if you'd join me."

When she nodded an okay, he said, "I'll see you in fifteen minutes," and proceeded up to his room. He showered and changed and wished he had time to polish his shoes. Something about the way she had agreed to join him seemed a little vague, and it bothered him.

Saila showed up a few minutes late, apologizing and looking different. To his surprise, she had put on a touch of lipstick. Their eyes met, and he realized she really had been looking forward to their date, but he also recognized something in her that *did* remind him of Lala. Perhaps she really was a New Type. There was only one reason he suspected this: there was something in her eyes he had never noticed before, something subjective, something that could not be explained logically. It was as if she had another aura about her, one darker, more urgent. He knew it wasn't malevolent, but whatever it was, Saila seemed different. Perhaps he had been blind all along, blinded by his impression of her as the bungler on ship, blinded by the childlike interest he had had in her ever since Side 7. He knew she had managed to lead the *Pegasus* survivors to safety before *Texas* had blown up. He knew that whatever image he had had of her in the past, it was time to revise it.

"Something the matter, Amuro?" she asked, looking at him oddly.

"Nothing . . . uh . . . I . . ." He started to say something but stopped. The most important thing at this point was just to sit down and calm down, but he was in a self-service dining room, with all the bothersome procedures it always entailed.

"Congratulations on your escape from *Texas*," he said as they started eating. "I heard all about how the *Pegasus* was put out of action."

"Thanks. But I wasn't on the ship at the end."

"You weren't?"

"That's right."

It had never occurred to him before. Did she mean that she had abandoned her post and fled? The rules were sometimes bent for the Waves in the military, but desertion was an offense for which men and women were judged equally.

"What happened?" he asked. "Some sort of New Type impulse grab you?" he feebly joked.

"I could feel the enemy," she said hesitatingly. "It felt like a powerful force. And I knew the whole crew would be in danger, so I left to locate an escape route from the colony."

"Wow."

She was feeding him a half lie. But it was true that

after parting with her brother Sha Aznable she had worked feverishly to help rescue the crew of the doomed *Pegasus*. In fact, as some of the crew members had later told Amuro, they had heard her voice mysteriously come out of nowhere.

"Did you know where the crew were when the ship finally went down?"

"No. I didn't know where *they* were, but they apparently knew where *I* was."

"See, you must be a New Type."

"I can't believe it myself. Do you really think this is the way New Type powers appear in people?"

"I did some research on New Types when I was on Side 6, Saila, and they're not supposed to be able to do anything supernatural. But if many can do what you did, I think the scientists'll have to rethink the whole concept."

"Don't read too much into what I did. The New Types that Zeon Zum Daikun spoke of were supposed to symbolize something much more universal, something that applied to all mankind."

"So?"

"It wasn't supposed to be someone who dashes off on a whim like me." She put her fork down on the table. "You know what? It's a one-sided affair for me."

A one-sided affair? What on earth did she mean? His ears immediately pricked up. Was she trying to tell him she was in love with someone?

"I have an older brother, Amuro. Someone I haven't seen for years and years. I sort of have a complex about the whole thing. Sometimes I have something like a seizure when I'm near him. I'm sorry, I know this all sounds weird."

An older brother? A seizure? Amuro was perplexed.

What in heaven's name was she talking about? What did this have to do with their discussion of New Types?

"It's like something suddenly goes off in my mind sometimes. Maybe in this case it helped me save the others."

"Saila, when you say 'seizure,' do you mean the sort of thing that might conceivably happen between two New Types if, say, their minds were on the same wavelength? The sort of thing that might suddenly expand their consciousness, even project it?" Amuro chose his words carefully, thinking of Lala Sun.

"You've quite a way with words, Ensign," she said. Then she looked into his eyes and added, "And you may be right."

"Think so?"

"Yes."

"I know you used the word 'seizure,' but I think you're really referring to a special ability, something that's dormant until activated by a sudden stimulus. Right?"

"Right. It's sort of like when—"

Amuro didn't need to hear the rest of her sentence. He had just realized something. "Like," he said, as if completing the sentence for her, "when you met your brother? Your brother Sha Aznable." It was incredible, but he knew exactly what she was trying to say.

Saila blanched.

"Forgive me," he quickly added. "Just my imagination."

"No," she replied hoarsely. "It's true. How'd you know?"

It was Amuro's turn to feel shocked. It was not the sort of connection, after all, that could be easily deduced. "That's a good question," he said. "I don't know. I wish I did, but I don't."

Sweat started to bead on his brow, and he raised his hand to wipe it. *How the hell could I know?* He didn't have the faintest idea. The whole conversation was starting to confuse him enormously. He looked at her. Maybe *she* had the answer. If anyone did, it would have to be Saila; he was sure she had something to do with what he had just sensed. Come to think of it, there was something similar about the aura he sensed around her and that which he had once sensed in Sha Aznable. But it was easy to make a logical connection after the fact. He waited for her to say something.

"As long as we're on this track," she continued haltingly, "you want to know something else? Sha's real name is Caspar Daikun, my real name is Artesia Daikun, and we're the children of Zeon Zum Daikun. Saila Mas is the name I took after my brother and I fled from the Zeon Archduchy to Earth. Well? How's that for a surprise?"

Amuro was stunned. He glanced around the room, and his nervous system went on 360-degree alert. It anyone overheard their conversation, there would be hell to pay. "This is not the place for that sort of talk, Saila," he cautioned.

"Maybe I made it all up," she countered with a weak smile.

"Saila! I honestly don't know if you did or not. But to me it's got to be real. It's the only way I can understand what I've been sensing in you."

"You think we're kindred spirits, Amuro?"

"For lack of a better word, yes. I've felt the same way with Sha, with Lala, and even with Kusko Al."

"*Lala? Kusko Al?* Who are they?"

"They're Zeon New Types. I had to fight Lala on *Texas*. And Kusko Al's probably the next one I'll face. I got to know her through the intelligence agency on Side 6. She's a New Type."

"So Zeon's really deploying New Types in combat?"

"Right," Amuro groaned, "while the Federation still thinks they're some sort of joke."

Kai Shiden suddenly entered the dining room with several mechamen and occupied the tables in a corner. "Yo, Ensign Amuro!" he called out. "Having a good time, eh? And the petty officer? How about a date with me tonight, sweetie?"

"Too bad, *Mister* Kai," Saila bantered back, her clear voice echoing through the dining hall. "I've already got one ensign here to keep me company, and that's enough."

Amuro's jaw dropped in amazement. As he stared at her in embarrassment, Kai's table erupted in laughter and wolf whistles. "Hey, Don Juan, the irresistible!" someone said in his direction. "It's not fair! You join our new ship late and then walk off with one of our prize Waves! What have you got to say for yourself?"

In the midst of the teasing, Saila turned to Amuro and joked. "Don't make me lose face now," she said. "Go along with it and make it up to them later. You know, buy them a drink or take them out to dinner."

"Me?" Amuro gulped.

"Sure. You. You *are* irresistible."

Something about the way she said it bothered Amuro. It reminded him of Kusko Al. And just when he thought of Kusko, the memory of Fra Bow washed over him. When he looked at Saila again, she was already standing up to leave.

* * *

"I think it's a little dangerous to write off the supreme commander as a mere fanatic," Lt. Sharia Bull whispered to Sha Aznable. "He does have some leadership qualities." The two men, along with Kusko Al, had gathered in an officer's music listening room on *Abowaku*. It was soundproofed, but they kept their voices low anyway.

"Aah, I agree," Sha said. "We can't overlook the fact that there is genuine support in Zeon for the dictatorship."

Sharia nodded in agreement but seemed to be pondering something.

Sha was beginning to rethink his opinion of the lieutenant. A New Type candidate who had arrived on *Abowaku* only six hours earlier, he was of medium build and height, not the type that stood out in a crowd. But there was something about the way he carried himself and the slightly hollowed look in his cheeks that spoke of incredible endurance. His résumé said he was twenty-eight, yet he looked far older. He seemed awfully cautious, but that was probably an important quality for someone in charge of the Jupiter transports.

"I'd say the real tragedy of our supreme commander," Kusko interjected, "is that his ambition exceeds his ability, wouldn't you?"

Kusko was striking in her military uniform. She wore it well, so well, in fact, that it almost looked as though the rather fashionable Zeon officers' uniforms had been specifically designed for her. But Sha was unimpressed. There was something about her that always irritated him. He had no problem with women in the force acting a little differently from the men—there was certainly no need for them to be exactly the same—but Kusko tended to ignore even the basic protocols of military hierarchy. And it was not just because she was something of a free spirit. Her parents had come from some place on Earth called Argentina but had divorced. She had moved to Side 3 as part of the forced emigration program to the space colonies. There was something self-destructive about her.

"Kusko," Sha cautioned, "we have to be careful not to speculate too much on his character." He wanted to put her in her place, but instead her eyes flashed in defiance. "We've got to keep track of what he's doing," he continued, "and collect more hard data on him. But we have to be careful. One wrong move and the people who are supposed to be our allies will do us in." He added the last statement because he feared more than anything else that she would leak word of their conversation to the wrong party. It seemed to work, for she fell silent.

"I may not be subordinate to Krishia forever," he continued, "but for now remember that we're under the command of Her Excellency and that without her we're doomed. Understand?"

Sharia softly asked, "You'll follow her as long as it fits in with your personal plans. Is that correct, sir?"

"Let's be blunt," Sha said. "I'll say yes, and you'll believe me, right?"

"Why are men always so power-hungry?" Kusko interjected again.

"Be careful," Sha cautioned her. "We didn't invite you in on this discussion."

"Maybe," she retorted with a laugh, "but you haven't asked me to leave, either. And I know why. Because you'd feel guilty if you did, right?"

"No, we're letting you stay because you're a New

Type, and we've got no choice. But there's no time to argue that point. There's something very important I've still got to confirm with Sharia."

"Go ahead. You've already said enough to make me a coconspirator."

To Sha's surprise, Sharia laughed and said, "She's right, Commander."

Sha and Sharia had originally planned to meet alone in the officers' private music listening room, but Kusko had somehow sensed their plans. Sha knew she had come more out of curiosity than anything else and felt obliged to let her stay, but it made him feel uneasy when Sharia mentioned Gren Zavi in her presence. Sharia was a New Type candidate specifically sent under Gren's orders. There was a distinct possibility that he might be a spy planted by Gren.

"I need some sort of guarantee from you," Sha said to Sharia. "Since there's a strong possibility that you may represent Gren's interest in this, how much can I trust you?"

"You have my word. Isn't that enough?"

"Perhaps yes. Perhaps no."

"The real reason I came here, Commander, is to confirm for myself that New Types actually existed. Frankly, I don't fully believe I have any New Type potential myself."

"You wanted to 'confirm for yourself'?"

"That's right, sir. Personally, I find the original theory of New Types espoused by Zeon Zum Daikun very appealing."

"He was an idealist, Sharia."

Zeon Zum Daikun had predicted that mankind would undergo a revolutionary transformation in outer space.

He believed that as men and women broke the boundaries of the planet Earth and moved farther and farther into space, making the entire universe their habitat, their consciousness would expand and become more universal. The farther they went, the more they would develop a powerful bond among themselves independent of physical distance. It would be an inevitable change and a logical step in the evolution of the human psyche.

The original New Type concept was simple and idealistic, but when war erupted, it took on an utterly new meaning. Perhaps because the military authorities of the Zeon Archduchy were so embroiled in war, they were the first to interpret it in their own way, latching on to the notion that New Types could be used for a more specific, immediate purpose—as humans with paranormal powers, as pilots with prescience, as weapons of war.

"I greatly admired Zeon Daikun," Sharia said. "It's a shame he didn't survive long enough to become more than just a revolutionary propagandist and visionary. He might have become the type of politician we really need today."

"No one can be everything," Sha said. "Besides, politicians with too much personal ambition make me nervous."

"True. That sort of thing can shorten a person's life. And if you always have a hidden agenda, people start to distrust you, too."

Sha's hands suddenly turned clammy. There was no way Sharia could possibly know his real identity, but he might have sensed something. His words were getting close to the danger zone. He was, without a doubt, a man with considerable intuition.

Sha replied as tactfully as possible, "I may outrank

you, Sharia, but you're older than I am and more experienced. I think I have a lot to learn from you.'' He didn't like saying it in front of Kusko Al, and it made him resent her presence all the more. Even before meeting Sharia, he had noted an obstinate masculine pride in himself.

Kusko spoke up as if sensing what the two men were thinking. ''I know I probably bug both of you. But you won't get much double-talk from me. Unlike you *men*, there's no hidden agenda in this girl.'' She meant to be sarcastic, but her words did not quite have the intended effect.

''All well and good,'' Sha said icily, ''but put your curiosity on hold. You know what it did to the cat, right? Sometimes it's better to be in the dark about these things. Sometimes it's dangerous to hook up with people in a situation like this. Be realistic about what you're getting into and conduct yourself in as responsible a fashion as possible.''

''Hmph,'' she replied petulantly. ''I can hardly change my basic personality, can I? In any case I wouldn't want to. I like the way I am, thank you.''

''In that case,'' Sharia said, ''you have to accept us the way we are, too, and be a good girl and occasionally leave the room. Frankly, I prefer women who don't pretend to be so intelligent.''

''Lieutenant!'' Kusko exclaimed.

Sha could not help smirking. Sharia was capable of a more barbed tongue than he would have ever imagined.

''We're not asking you to change your personality,'' Sharia continued, ''but it does sometimes create problems for us. We have to worry. We might say something you don't like. How do we know you won't betray us to the Zavi family?''

''Well, if that's the way you feel, why'd you say all that stuff in front of me?''

''You gave the answer earlier. We set you up as a coconspirator. Sha Aznable accepted Sharia Bull, the spy sent by Supreme Commander Gren, as a partner in his plans. In the future he's going to destroy Krishia Zavi and eventually the supreme commander himself.''

''You both must be *dreaming*!''

''If you think so, keep your nose out of it,'' Sha said. ''This is our business. The fact that Sharia Bull came as Gren's spy to find out what Krishia's up to, the fact of my plotting . . . forget everything you heard. Understand?''

''I can't believe the way you men act,'' Kusko retorted.

''We're at war, Kusko.''

Kusko kicked off the floor and left the room, slamming the door behind her. Sharia turned to Sha. ''Let's head over to the base bar,'' he said with a smile, ''and have a drink to clear the air a bit. There are some girls over there who are a little less trouble.''

''Sounds fine. To tell the truth, I'm not even sure myself why I have such trouble getting along with her.''

''That's just the way people are, Commander. You said it earlier. No one can be everything to everyone.''

The two men turned off the lights and left the listening room. From outside the window, the moonlight streamed inside. Earth was out of sight.

It was a good thing women had such warm, smooth skin, Amuro thought, as he spread his right hand over the gentle mound of Saila's breast. Then he remembered what someone had once told him—that sleeping people have nightmares if something weighs upon their chests—and removed his hand, reluctantly letting it drift down to her side. His eyes lingered on the gentle shape of her breasts and the delicate outline of her nipples.

It was a violation of military regulations for a woman to be in a male officer's quarters at night, but it happened all the time and was never punished anymore. Nearly thirty percent of the Federation Forces were now Waves, and liaisons were overlooked as long as the following basic guidelines were observed: Trainees could not be involved, the interaction could not be during a time of combat and had to take place in a private room, and everyone had to be in his or her original assigned quarters for lights-out and reveille. The last rule was one of the reasons that in some quarters there was a considerable amount of coming and going ten minutes after the official lights-out time.

Attitudes toward sex had changed radically in the Space Age, but most people still looked askance at those who engaged in promiscuous activity. Inappropriate behavior often resulted in harsh criticism from fellow crew members, coupled with accusations of being a "playboy" or "playgirl," terms with highly negative overtones. When Saila had first entered his room, she had grinned and said, "I passed Mirai on the way here, but she doesn't suspect anything. Some of our pals back there in the dining hall probably feel jilted, though, so don't forget to be nice to them."

"Oh." That was all Amuro had managed to say. After that he remembered little. She had received him, and he had felt vaguely dissatisfied after it was all over. Then she had said with a giggle, *"If I'm ever assigned a private room, you can come visit me."* That had been ten minutes earlier. Now he could tell by her breathing that she was fast asleep. It was funny. He had first thought she had come to him specifically to talk about Sha Aznable. But to his surprise, it seemed she had just come to sleep with him. She had wrapped him in her exquisitely long limbs and hadn't mentioned her brother's name once.

There was definitely something unnerving about the ways of women, he thought, wondering if Fra Bow was the same way. Then the fatigue from a long day caught up with him, and he fell asleep in the warmth of Saila's body, marveling at how complex humans were.

He awoke abruptly to the sound of Saila sobbing quietly, her face buried in a pillow and her shoulders shaking. "Saila, what is it?" he asked.

"Amuro," she sobbed almost inaudibly. "I'm sorry . . . I'm sorry."

He gingerly placed his hand on her back and, as she kept weeping, began gently massaging her. Then, to his surprise, she suddenly rolled over, jumped out of bed, and ran to the shower. It happened so fast, he only saw her white limbs flash for a second in the darkness.

He roused himself, shocked. From the shower he could hear the water blasting her skin. He placed his hand on the impression her body had left on the bed and felt the residual warmth. He swore softly and bit his thumbnail.

Ten minutes later the sound of the shower stopped. The door to the bathroom opened, and Saila emerged, a bath towel wrapped around her torso. She walked straight over to him and announced, "Well? Think I'm pretty?"

"Very," he said.

"Thanks." She sat down next to him and added hesitatingly, "I mean it. And on a totally different subject, about tonight."

He was absorbed in the beautiful lines of her neck and back, but he thought he knew exactly what she was going to say—that they would not be able to sleep together again. To his amazement she suddenly announced, "I love my brother, Amuro, but he's gone too far. He seems to have delusions about what can be done with New Types, and I'm afraid he might do something horrible. If you meet him, I want you . . . to kill him." Then, seeing his shock, she added, "It hurts me to say it, but I mean it. I can't stand to think of my brother as someone playing God. I'd rather see him dead."

"I don't kill people for personal reasons," he replied, his voice rising in anger. "Is this why you slept with me?"

"No, no," she moaned softly. "It doesn't have anything to do with it."

"Listen, Saila. You're a complicated person. I've known you as the young blonde on Side 7, as the *Pegasus*'s communications officer, and now even as Artesia, child of the late Zeon Zum Daikun. But to me there's only one real Saila. You're always Saila, and I don't like the Saila I see now."

"I'm sorry, Amuro. But I almost never have a chance to talk to you, so when I'm with you like this, everything gets mixed up and you wind up misunderstanding me. It's not the way you think it is!"

"Maybe not. Maybe I'll never meet Sha in combat again. Who knows? *I* may be killed first. Either way, what you just said to me is *taboo*."

"Amuro, I don't think you can understand because you've never had a brother you really love!"

"I hope I never love anyone so much I want them dead."

He suddenly felt thirsty and stood up and walked to the bathroom to get a drink. He was stark naked, but he didn't care. He wished Saila would leave and decided to kill some time by taking a shower. But even afterward he could sense she was still in the room. Sure enough, when he emerged, she was wrapped in a blanket on his bed, lying face up, her eyes open, staring at the ceiling.

"I'm sorry," she said. "Let's go back to sleep."

He thought about sleeping alone on the sofa in the room, but her warm body was too tempting, and besides, it was *his* room and *his* bed. He lay down beside her, and before he slipped into sleep, he felt her hand reach out and gently touch his waist.

CHAPTER 13

CONTACT

Earth Federation scouts had detected a change in Zeon activity. Krishia's forces, the survivors of the *Granada* battle, and other support warships had previously been observed converging around *Abowaku*. But now there were ships from entirely different units moving under full speed in the opposite direction, toward *Solomon*. General Revil and his top officers puzzled over the new information.

"Sir, it looks like Vice Admiral Dozzle Zavi's mobile attack unit is trying to link up with the Zeon reserves on *Solomon* and stage an attack on *LH*."

"What should we do, sir? We don't have enough ships to divert some to another position."

"Are you absolutely certain Dozzle's headed for *Solomon*?"

"Yessir, and if he links up with the other ships there, they'll form a fleet that could easily take on *LH*. That means the *Abowaku* forces will also probably come out in a feint maneuver and try to take *LH* in a pincer attack."

"We've got to be able to support *LH* somehow. We've got three divisions on Luna II that could help."

"Yes, sir."

"It's a tough call. We don't have any solid proof Dozzle will attack *LH*. But on the other hand, the Zeon forces are as much in the dark about our plans as we are about theirs. This is where Zavi family rivalries get interesting. It looks like the Zeon high command has equally divided their forces between Dozzle and Krishia Zavi so neither loses face."

General Revil made light of the situation, but he was troubled by the lack of information on the true extent of the Zeon forces converging on *LH*. The whole business was distracting him from his own plans. The twenty-square-meter 3D display projected on the ceiling above him showed the estimated positions of both enemy and friendly forces in red and green flashing lights and did a particularly good job of representing the moon. He looked up at it and muttered, "Where's the focus of Zeon's military strength now? That's what I need to know. Where's their New Type unit?" He was convinced Zeon had not yet totally committed its New Type unit, and he was certain it was not the centerpiece of their current strategy. He even suspected that much of the talk of Zeon New Types was simply rumor, perhaps intentionally planted by spies.

"Abowaku," he whispered to himself. "Hmm . . . And we know that several ships from Side 6 have recently docked there."

He was even more worried by information he had received about Zeon's *Mahar* colony. A flurry of activity had apparently taken place there, perhaps in relation to an evacuation of the entire cylinder.

"Any evidence an evacuation has been completed?" he asked.

No one knew yet.

After spending the night with Amuro, the first thing Saila said was, "If you're a real New Type, Amuro, it's a dream come true for me. Maybe you wish I'd never said what I did about my brother earlier, but it's too late. I said it, and I can't help it if you hate me for it."

Still sitting on the bed with his back to her, he replied, "I just don't understand it. I don't have a brother. But I don't think it's the sort of thing anyone should ever say."

"Maybe so," she said, suddenly gloomy.

Amuro turned around and looked at her. She had just finished fastening her brassiere. *How beautiful she is,* he thought. As if sensing him, she smiled faintly. He stood up, hugged her, kissed the nape of her neck, and drank deeply of her scent. There was always something vague and unsettling between men and women, and surely that was the problem between him and Saila. Her earlier statement had been so outrageous, he decided that it must have stemmed from a twisted desire to *save* her brother. That was the only way he could possibly interpret it. And as for her remark about his being a New Type, well, he couldn't really understand the connection. She probably just needed a man to help her forget the whole unpleasantness with her brother, and any man who could keep her attention would do. Amuro was not even sure if he filled the bill on that score. The more his New Type potential developed, the more prone to self-delusion he seemed to be becoming.

Saila sighed deeply and embraced him. He held her tightly around the waist and noted how slender and delicate she seemed. He wished he were more experienced, more of a man, and knew better what to do. She groaned, and he realized he had squeezed her too hard. "Sorry," he apologized, cursing his clumsiness.

"Enemy forces at 186 degrees, 10 minutes! Elevation thirty-three degrees twenty-six minutes! Stage one alert!"

Speakers blared throughout the Federation's *LH* moon base, letting the defenders know that Zeon's ships would enter missile and beam cannon range within ten minutes. Amuro and his fellow pilots had just returned from a second training mission when the next announcement came: *"Open launch deck doors! All crew don Normal Suits!"*

The *Pegasus*'s deck hatch doors opened. Amuro hooked a lift-grip and sped along at maximum speed through a passageway leading directly to the deck and then used his inertia to leap up to the new Gundam model Mobile Suit. The moon had gravity, but it was easy to jump four or five meters. He knew the *Pegasus* was already moving, because through its open front hatch he could see the walls of the *LH* moon port slide downward.

From inside the Gundam cockpit, he yelled into his microphone, "This is G3! Ensign Amuro Rey, ready for launch!"

The communications monitor above his main display flickered to life, and Saila's voice emerged from its speaker: *"Pegasus exiting port area in twenty seconds. Launch after confirming clearance!"*

"Roger! G3 now launching!"

"Amuro?" Saila was so surprised that she unintentionally violated takeoff protocol by calling out infor-

mally—there was a strict rule against launching Mobile Suits before the *Pegasus* completely cleared the port area, and it looked like Amuro was about to break it.

Through the open launch hatch in front of the Gundam, Amuro watched the walls of port slip by faster and faster. He waited for the right instant and then yelled, "Enemy approaching! G3 now launching!" He fired the main engine under him, and it responded with a roar that reverberated through his spine.

"G3! Ensign Amuro launching!" He heard Saila confirm his launch and relay the information to Brite. In the background he thought he heard the skipper say something negative, but he was not about to dwell on it. He stepped down on the middle launch pedal and felt a mild *g* force as all sixteen meters of the giant Gundam Mobile Suit surged forward on the launch catapult. The instant it kicked off the catapult, he fired the backpack verniers and put them on full thrust, and the Suit began a slow climb, squeezing through the eighty-meter gap between the *Pegasus* and the inside walls of the moon base. In seconds he had checked his ceiling display and confirmed that he had the correct attitude and trajectory to clear the port. Then he checked his beam rifle and the arm that held it for full range of movement and checked the integrity of the energy circuits. Then he released the safety on his weapons systems. When he next glanced at his main monitor, he had safely cleared the moon surface.

"Godspeed, Ensign Amuro!" Saila's voice came through, but when Amuro turned to look at the minimonitor where her face normally appeared, Minovski interference had already broken up her image. Her next words were unintelligible, but he didn't have time to listen, anyway. The static was so distracting that he

turned it off. From that point on he had to locate the enemy with the naked eye. He switched the cockpit's eight observation displays to maximum telescopic mode for a 360-degree panorama.

What the—

To his horror, what looked like an enemy Mobile Suit was rapidly descending behind him toward the moon surface. Even worse, the *LH* base had not yet fired a single cannon or missile in defense. One cardinal rule of military strategy was that once a lone MS broke through a defensive perimeter, it was almost impossible to stop, but none of the Federation Forces seemed to have even noticed.

He spun the Gundam around and gave chase at high speed. The *g*s pushed him back into his seat, and the thrill of an impending fight made his spine tingle. He eased off on the left and right levers and told himself to slow down, be careful. The enemy Suit swung into view directly in front of him, and it was definitely a Zak, but faster than any he had seen before. To his dismay, it was still plunging unchallenged straight toward a corner of the *LH*. Worse yet, he realized it might only be a decoy. The enemy sometimes deployed Zaks at that stage of attack, but they rarely sent out only one.

There was not a second to be wasted. He fired a single blast from his beam rifle. The enemy Suit was too far away for a direct hit, but the beam would help alert the Federation defenders. As he expected, the Suit returned his fire, but he ignored it. He twisted his MS ninety degrees and checked the heavens unfolding above him. Amid the static from Minovski interference, he could overhear panic in the communications transmissions from *LH*. The people down on the base had never in their wildest dreams imagined such a sudden attack, even from a scout unit.

The two Gun Cannons from the *Pegasus* finally caught up with him, but he couldn't help grumbling when he noticed that the new GM pilots—Ensign Sarkus and Kria—were late. In Mobile Suit battles, machines normally advanced in formation until the enemy was directly engaged; from then on it was essentially every man for himself. There were, of course, some basic tactics employed—most of which were based on conventional dogfighting experience—but there were no hard-and-fast rules. MS combat was a relatively new type of warfare with no real military model to follow, and it tended to quickly devolve into close-quarter combat.

Amuro slowed down when he finally saw the *Pegasus* pulling along his port side. He wanted at all costs to avoid being separated from his own forces and accidentally destroying a friendly ship. As he watched, a *Salamis*-class cruiser rose up on either side, and the lead one moved straight forward. Its goal was clear: to protect the heart of the *LH* moon base.

"Don't overexpose yourself!" he yelled at the lead cruiser over his mike, but it was too late. He sensed a light ahead of them, coming faster and faster, almost leaping out toward him. It was a light he had experienced before, when fighting the Red Comet and when fighting Lala Sun in her Mobile Armor. It was a thin, glowing beam of light traveling at great speed. And then he saw the flares of five or six rocket engines spinning, coming closer and closer.

"Damn! I've seen this before! I know what this is!" He swore under his breath, leveled his beam rifle in front of him, and fired. He knew the blast was wasted.

It scorched through the blackness of space, but the things he was aiming at were far too fast. They leapt out of the way and continued to plunge toward the lead *Salamis*-class cruiser.

The next blast from his beam rifle finally struck home—one of the attacking objects burst into a ball of white light in the blackness. But only then did the lead *Salamis*-class cruiser seem to realize it was the target of the attack and commence defensive fire. The rocket-propelled objects evaded the barrage and made a beeline toward the ship.

One of the easiest ways to overwhelm a defense is with numbers. Amuro picked off another of the objects, but that was as much as he could do. Several missiles plunged into the cruiser's bridge, and after a few paralyzing seconds of nothingness it was enveloped in flames. Then the flames mushroomed into a ball of white light that illuminated the surface of the moon below.

Amuro knew he was confronting the same weapon Lala Sun had used—the Elmeth and its Bits. The weaving engine flares were from the multiple supporting units, armed with either a beam cannon or nuclear warheads and controlled from the Elmeth despite the heavy Minovski concentrations. Amuro knew from prior experience that the Bits were not radio-controlled, that somehow Lala Sun, the pilot, had been able to control them with her brain waves. What he and the Earth Federation Forces did not yet know was that the system depended on a new interface device, called a psychom, which had magnified and projected her will.

Another Lala Sun! Amuro remembered what Lt. List Hayashida had said about Zeon's plans for a New Type unit. The Flanagan Agency had clearly been more successful than the Earth Federation had ever suspected.

They can't possibly have very many of these things, though. He tried to reassure himself, straining to see better in the area of space where the flares had appeared. Unlike the time he had encountered Lala, he still could not "feel" anything from the pilot of the main component in the system. After pondering for a second, he decided it must be because of the distance involved. There was one other possibility, but it was too terrifying to consider.

Kai, Hayato, and the two GM pilots deployed their Suits in a horizontal formation on either side of *Pegasus II*, and Amuro yelled into his mike as loudly as possible at the two Gun Cannons: "We're under attack by enemy New Types! Make sure GM 324 and 325 stay to our rear!" Almost immediately, he heard Kai parrot his words in shock. *"Enemy New Types?"*

There was no time to reply. Amuro had already spotted Zeon Suits above and to his right—six of them and all a model he had never seen before, deployed in what he recognized as a "spear" formation. There was no sign of the Elmeth-Bits system. Before he could get a good look at them, they plunged forward, attacking a squad of *Salamis*-class cruisers to the *Pegasus*'s starboard that were riding cover over the Federation's third *White Base*-class ship, the *Thoroughbred*. Six Federation GMs came soaring up in the *Thoroughbred*'s defense, but it was obvious that their pilots were green and outclassed. Worse yet, Amuro could tell that the new model Zeon Suits were even faster than Zaks.

"Kai! Hayato!" he yelled. "Don't leave the *Pegasus* unprotected!" He spun his Gundam to the right and put it into a dive. There was no way to save the cruisers, and at that point he wasn't even certain he could help the *Thoroughbred*, but he had to try. His gray Suit streaked through the black space above the moon as he desperately attempted to cut off the enemy.

The new model Zeon Suits had flared waists that gave them a less threatening skirted appearance, but Amuro knew it was an illusion. The new design probably hid the nozzles of new, more powerful rocket engines, which in turn accounted for the increased speed over the old Zaks. When he saw a ball of white light flare in space again, he knew one of the enemy Suits had already scored a direct hit on a *Salamis*-class cruiser.

"You'll pay for that," he yelled while lining up the sights on his beam rifle with the cross hairs on his main monitor. For an instant the lead Zeon Suit seemed to waver.

"Sensed me, eh?" he said, surprised. In a fraction of a second he shifted his aim to the next Suit in line and pulled the trigger. A narrow band of light streaked out of his gun barrel and struck the enemy Suit, which was still illuminated by the earlier Salamis's explosion. Yet another equally large ball of light mushroomed in the same area, and the enemy formation shifted to a course that took them below it, out of Amuro's view. As he watched, the *Thoroughbred* emerged shuddering from the light, dropping in altitude toward the surface of the moon.

"You're reacting too slow!" he yelled at the Federation ship. The *Thoroughbred* had almost met the same fate the cruiser had earlier. At the rate things were going, the enemy Suits would continue their hit and run tactics, swoop close to the surface of the moon, dodge *LH*'s air defenses, and then disengage. And in the interim they would destroy a couple more Federation ships.

Amuro nonetheless chose not to pursue the formation. He was more worried about the Elmeth he had encountered earlier; it was a far more formidable rival. He turned the Gundam around and positioned himself under the left wing of the *Pegasus*. Kai, in his C108 Gun Cannon initiated skin talk with him.

"I can't see any enemy above us, Amuro," Kai said. "What's going on? You're supposed to be the New Type around here."

"They're incredibly fast. And they've got a new type of Suit. I think they're using beam rifles!"

"Did you see them?"

"Hell, yes!"

"Well, dammit, I couldn't. I saw something that looked like a Zak, but it was gone before I could be sure."

"Kai! What am I gonna do? I depend on you! Your Gun Cannon's supposed to play the main role in long-range support."

"Go easy on me, pal."

"Whoa!" Amuro suddenly exclaimed. He felt a ricochetlike sound. It was distinct but not physical and neither discernibly high nor low in tone. It seemed to reverberate not in his ears but directly on his brain stem. And he wasn't the only one to sense it; Kai, Hayato, and all the others in the area apparently did, too. Then it happened again. It was powerful enough to make all who heard it tremble in fear.

Saila was manning the communications panel on the *Pegasus* bridge when she first heard it. Fearing her headset was somehow preventing her from telling where the sound was coming from, she tore it off her head and stared around the room as if looking for the source. Brite, in the captain's seat, turned around and gaped at her.

"Was that caused by a failure in the communications system?" he asked.

"I can't tell, skipper."

Mirai, manning the helm, turned to Saila and exclaimed, "I heard it too!" Then both women simultaneously arrived at the same conclusion. "It's coming from outside the ship," they announced.

"Outside?" Brite, following their gaze, stared through the bridge window at the space in front of them. All he could see was the usual: millions of stars staring back at him. Then he noticed the two GM Mobile Suits attached to *Pegasus II*. They had moved two thousand meters out in front of the ship, apparently anticipating trouble.

Saila couldn't sit in front of the communications panel any longer. She stood up, kicked away her chair, and ran over to the bridge window. Because the sound she "heard" seemed to trail off in a specific direction, she looked upward.

"Ensign Mirai!" she exclaimed. "There's a light . . ." She knew none of the others would be able to see it. She wasn't even a hundred percent sure she hadn't imagined it herself.

"What are you talking about?" Brite demanded.

"Mirai! It's coming at us . . . at about one o'clock!"

In response Mirai immediately spun the helm, and in so doing violated a basic rule of the ship. Brite was technically only a junior grade lieutenant, but he was still captain of the ship, and *he* was the one who was supposed to issue orders. Mirai had acted unilaterally.

But that same instant Brite saw the Gundam and Gun Cannons swoop into view, firing their beam rifles and 28-centimeter shoulder cannons. And then he saw the light of three explosions mushroom in the area Saila had pointed to earlier. The filter on the shellproofed glass of the bridge windows automatically activated, and in the reduced light he finally spotted something else—what looked like six homing missiles—streaking toward the *Pegasus*. "So that's what they were talking about!" he exclaimed.

"Hard to starboard!" he yelled. "Give me a curtain of defensive fire!" He knew there was no time to execute his orders properly, but luckily sniping blasts from the Gundam's beam rifle took out three of the objects bearing down on them. The bridge rocked from the closest explosions, and then special protective barriers were activated on all ship windows. With the main bridge window view blocked, Brite concentrated his gaze on a large horizontally elongated, rhomboid-shaped monitor above it, which now displayed the same view. On it he saw the immediate light from the blasts diffuse, and residual particles flash and fade.

"Think they were homing missiles?" he asked Saila. They had seemed to cut an arc through space.

"I don't know, sir," she replied. "But I don't think so." Before the window barriers had completely retracted, she began to scan the heavens in front of the ship visually.

"The Gundam's moving out, sir," she announced.

"Good! Let him!" Brite replied. "But tell the Gun Cannons and the GMs to strengthen their defense of the ship." Something was happening that he did not understand. Amuro, Saila, Mirai, and the others were reacting on their own. He was the skipper, and it was frustrating, but he know that for the sake of the ship's survival he would have to go along with what they did.

Saila relayed the orders and felt a new respect for her commanding officer. He was the ship's captain. She was a relatively raw recruit, a lowly second-class petty officer. He could have thrown the book at her for acting on her own, but he seemed to be taking it all in stride. Things were happening beyond his immediate comprehension, but he was nonetheless capable of deducing the proper response. He was either a man with enormous leadership potential, she thought, or perhaps even someone with New Type potential. General Revil had overcome considerable opposition in the civilian and military hierarchy to appoint Brite skipper of the *Pegasus II*, but Brite's performance now, Saila concluded, more than justified the effort.

Twelve small monitors on her communications panel were dedicated to Mobile Suits in the area. As she relayed Brite's orders to the four Suits still hugging close to the *Pegasus*, she kept an eye on the one that normally showed Amuro. He was so far away that it was filled with static, but sometimes for a few fleeting seconds she could distinguish his form in the darkened Gundam cockpit. She knew she was probably the last thing on his mind right now, but that was the way men were in combat. She was thinking about him not because she had more time on her hands than he did but because of a strange tension she felt. His image on her screen was always the same size, but he was physically rapidly distancing himself from her—she could *feel* the increased separation. Was she being oversensitive? She didn't think so. It was simply that every once in a while she couldn't help thinking of him hurtling through space, hunting for the *thing* that had targeted them. What was it? She recalled the mysterious sensation she had felt earlier—first an indescribable tone that had pierced her brow, then a glowing streak she could "see" deep in her mind. The line of light it had formed still lingered, and she felt she could almost trace it back to its source in space. And she knew that was where Amuro was headed. He was plunging into the unknown, doing something terribly dangerous but terribly important. The more she thought about it, the more she admired him. He had the same mysterious inner strength she had observed earlier in her captain.

Brite interrupted her thought with a command. "Saila! Tell everyone manning laser-sensors to ignore the others for the moment and concentrate on Amuro!"

"Yessir," she replied. Brite clearly seemed to know what was going on.

Mirai, at the helm, turned and queried, "What do you think's out there, skipper?"

Staring straight ahead, he answered without hesitating, "A real New Type. Mirai, Saila . . . you both saw something earlier, didn't you?"

Saila felt she had finally become a true member of the *Pegasus II* core crew. And despite everything else that was going on, she felt happy.

As with many regions near Earth, the area surrounding the moon was contaminated with debris from the ravages of war. Chunks of landfill and sections of former colony structures—objects often over a hundred meters in diameter—floated incongruously, randomly, in orbit.

Amuro Rey skillfully made his Gundam leap over one such obstacle and then finally spotted what he was looking for—the same machine Lala Sun had once piloted, an Elmeth. He swore under his breath, trying not to think how many more of the things he might soon confront, and then saw something streak toward him. But it was not the flare of a rocket. The Elmeth had fired its beam cannon at him. Without bothering to line up his sights, he squeezed the trigger, and several bands of light from his beam rifle converged on the enemy machine, but it leapt effortlessly out of the way. He had no time to try to establish any empathic communication with the pilot; the waves of thought he felt streaming toward him were too unidirectional, too powerful, too insistent, and too unyielding.

Concentrating, he squeezed the trigger again, hoping for a single knockout blow. He had already learned enough about the Elmeth's performance from seeing its reaction to his first blast to know that he had to act fast or it would kill him. To his dismay, it evaded his second attack, too. And his third. The enemy pilot appeared to possess a mysterious latent power.

Two more beams streaked out from the Elmeth toward him. Thanks to the Gundam's new magnetic coating, he was able to evade them, but he knew he was being outmaneuvered. A new, unfamiliar anger suddenly welled up inside him. He raged against the faceless Elmeth pilot for cooperating with Zeon. It was because of such cooperation that military men on both sides were starting to consider New Types instruments of war. He wanted to scream. *New Types aren't weapons! They're humans! You're supposed to be like Lala Sun, capable of a new communion of thought!*

The more emotional Amuro became, the faster he wanted to move and the more he wanted to close in on the Elmeth and destroy it. He slipped by some more space debris, slid sharply to the right, and there it was again. With his left monitor clearly showing the rear of the enemy machine, he kept it in his line of fire, and the instant it seemed to notice him, he pulled the trigger. First he thought he had scored a direct hit, but after the initial whoosh of light he realized with disappointment that the Elmeth had only been grazed and probably had received only minor damage. It seemed to stagger in the light but then proceeded to hide itself in the remains of a destroyed colony.

Amuro knew it was time to abandon his pursuit. A heavy, oppressive sensation began to form in his subconscious, quickly transforming itself into physical fear. Something was coming at him from behind. It was *he*! *He* was coming! There was no mistaking it. It was Sha—the *Red Comet*! Sure enough, he glanced up at his left rearview monitor and saw readouts in both corners indicating relative distance and estimated point of contact with an approaching object. But this was not a video game simulation. He needed more than numbers. He needed visual confirmation. He spun the Gundam around 180 degrees and spotted the enemy Suit. But Sha was not piloting the red Zak he had expected. His new model MS had a flared skirtlike construction where its legs would have been and was painted a dark color to blend in with the blackness of space. Its mono-eye flashed as it plunged straight toward him.

Amuro swore softly: *"Don't underestimate me, Sha."* He adjusted his sights and felt a renewed sense of oppression. His opponent was angry and—he realized with some surprise—probably as desperate as he was himself. But Amuro didn't realize that his own emotions were being triggered by a type of empathy, that he was already unconsciously adapting to his enemy's mood, and that if he weren't careful, the empathy itself could cause his destruction.

The skirted Zeon Suit proceeded in a straight line and then, as if sensing Amuro's weakness, suddenly fired its beam rifle. A cluster of beams streaked toward Amuro, but he had already shifted his own Suit to the right and positioned his shield in front of him with its right arm. The next nanosecond the main beam creased him, and the glowing particles on its periphery blasted thousands of invisible holes in the shield. The Gundam body shuddered, its mechanical components strained to the limit.

Even in his new Rik Dom MS, Sha still relied on his old hit-and-run tactics. Seconds later he slipped by the Gundam's left side and fired. But Amuro fired at exactly the same instant. Incredibly, the particle beams from their respective rifles collided head-on, and a ball of white light equal to that of an exploding warship mushroomed in space and then faded.

"He's faster than I thought," Sha swore. He knew that if the Gundam had been caught in the middle of the light, all the armor in the world would not have saved it. He had visually sighted and attacked the enemy Suit, but it had demonstrated astounding speed and agility in its evasive action and counterattack. For a second he wondered if the Gundam before him was really the same one he had encountered in battle before. Its fuselage was no longer white but had a light gray look that made it seem more formidable than before. He grinned despite himself at the psychological effect a mere color change could create. And the pilot? He considered the notion that it might be the same young kid

he had faced before on *Texas* but quickly abandoned the idea. There was no way of precisely knowing the final outcome of the Gundam's showdown with Lala's Elmeth on *Texas*, but there was also no way, he told himself, that its pilot could possibly have escaped the subsequent explosion of the colony cylinder. He himself had escaped only by the skin of his teeth, and at that point he had already intuitively known that Lala Sun was dead. He recalled the whole affair with particular bitterness, for during her last moments he knew she had had someone other than him in her heart. And her death had made the idea that the enemy Mobile Suit and its pilot might have survived almost too cruel to contemplate, for it would mean she had fought and died in vain. Except for the pilot of the original white Mobile Suit, he had received no intelligence information on the existence of any other Federation New Types. He desperately wished he knew exactly what had happened.

In the meantime he shielded his Rik Dom behind some floating debris and checked for any movement to his rear. "Where's Sharia Bull?" he muttered. He trusted the lieutenant and was convinced he was the real thing. In terms of the man's ability to fly in formation and the way he had evaded the Federation beam blast earlier, it was entirely possible that he possessed even greater skills than he, Sha, the seasoned combat veteran, did.

Just as he feared, less than forty kilometers to his rear he saw several streaks of light in the blackness. He put his Rik Dom into a jump and sprang from his cover. To his astonishment, he nearly collided with the Gundam, whose pilot was just as taken aback as he was. It all happened so fast that as the two Suits slipped by each other neither pilot had time to properly aim his beam rifle or bazooka. Sha swore and fired even though he knew it was useless, and the Gundam pilot did the same. But then something different happened to the Gundam. As Sha watched, beams fired by Sharia Bull rained down on the Gundam from above and to the left, but when he turned back to look at the Federation Suit, it had already evaded them by slipping sideways and taking cover behind 100-meter-long rock. The rock caught a beam blast and exploded in fragments, but that did not help Sha, for in the explosion the enemy Suit suddenly vanished from his view.

He swore again. *"Where in hell is Kusko Al and her Elmeth?"* She had always seemed overconfident. He had no way of knowing she had been hit by the Gundam earlier.

Amuro Rey was getting nervous. There were two skirted Zeon Suits after him, and something made him suspect that both of their pilots were New Types. He had to make sure they didn't get near Kai and Hayato, and if at all possible destroy them before his comrades entered the combat zone. He knew things weren't going in his favor. He turned away from the moon, scanned his observation displays, and saw two more mushrooming balls of white light from exploding Federation ships in the area. It seemed incredible that only four or five enemy Suits could wreak so much damage.

He knew what he had to do and knew that only he could do it. His ego was egging him on, but he also knew he would need every ounce of confidence he could find simply to confront the pilots in Zeon's New Type unit. Keeping one eye on Sha's skirted Suit below him, he turned and saw the Suits that had rained beams on him a second earlier. To his horror, instead of two, there were now three. Where had he miscalculated?

He pulled the trigger, and the muzzle of his beam rifle flared, but the result was unexpected. He had aimed at the lead Suit, but it had executed a perfect evasion maneuver, and his beam had scored a direct hit on the second Suit in line instead. His elation with a hit was quickly tempered with fear. Why, he nearly screamed aloud, had the lead Suit been able to avoid him? Who the hell was piloting it? It certainly was no ordinary person, and it might be an opponent even more formidable than Sha Aznable.

He fired two more bursts of beams. Incredibly, the lead Suit evaded him again. What on earth was its faceless pilot trying to do? He wanted to scream *"Stop!"* He wanted desperately to tell him true New Types wouldn't lend their powers to an enemy as detestable as the Zavi family. He was furious.

As his Gundam streaked through the void, he saw fire below him from Kai and Hayato's Gun Cannons converge on the skirted Zeon Suits. It was ineffective, and he knew it would only make things worse. Sure enough, both the Federation fleet guns and the ground-based defenses below suddenly concentrated a furious barrage of fire right on the area he was in.

He yelled, *"Hey! Don't forget I'm here!"* but knew he probably would have done the same thing in their position. Within the space of a dozen minutes nearly ten Federation ships had been incinerated. The junior officers manning the moon base missiles and the ships' guns were almost duty bound to fire if they so much as thought they saw the enemy. In the midst of the barrage he strained to keep an eye on the Rik Doms and hoped he wouldn't be hit.

* * *

Sha finally gave the order to retreat. His men had done enough fighting for the day. They had obtained valuable data on the performance of the Elmeth and new Rik Dom machines in combat, and both Kusko Al and Sharia Bull had managed to get in a little on-the-job training. To stay longer in an area so clearly controlled by the enemy would be tantamount to suicide. He pulled out of the area, and the surviving Zeon Suits followed him, trailed by withering fire from the Earth Federation Forces that illuminated the blackness.

With the attack on the Federation's *LH* moon base finally over, the *Pegasus II* returned to port, where, to the crew's surprise, they found they had all been promoted an entire rank. General Revil, acting on his own conviction, had decided a promotion was necessary for them to function as an official New Type Corps, and the General Staff at Jaburo on Earth, realizing that he was staking his career and life on the new strategy, had decided to humor him. They had apparently even considered advancing the crew two ranks in the hierarchy, but Revil had balked.

"If we don't promote them," the brass reportedly had said, "their ranks will be out of sync with those of the crews on other warships. How can Brite Noa function as skipper if he's only a lieutenant?"

"They're all too young," Revil had replied. "It'd go to their heads. They know what they're in for, and I need them to think clearly."

At around eleven o'clock mean time, Brite returned to the *Pegasus* from a war council on the base. Although none of the core crew members had been ordered to do so, they had gathered in the armory almost as if on cue and were waiting for him.

Brite, now a full lieutenant, turned to Amuro and joked, "If it gets too hard for us to synchronize our activities with you, mister, we might have to put you in charge of tactical operations, eh?"

"Only if I have the appropriate qualifications and talent, sir." Amuro grinned back. He himself had been promoted to junior grade lieutenant, as had Kai Shiden, Hayato Kobayashi, and Mirai Yashima.

Sleggar Row, the gunnery specialist and already a junior grade lieutenant, griped, "Am I the only one who didn't get promoted just 'cause I joined later than the rest of you?"

"It's all a fluke, Sleggar," Brite answered, as if consoling him. "They only did this to make my job easier as skipper of the ship." Then, turning to Saila, he said, "And you, you're a petty officer first class now, so have a seat along with the rest and listen to what I'm about to say. The general was extremely interested in learning more about the enemy's raid on *LH* today, but I couldn't fill him in on the details at the meeting because so many others were in attendance. One thing's clear, though. The Gundam moved out too fast."

Brite sipped on a cup of coffee when he said this and then glanced at Amuro. "It's too bad we can't depend on radio transmissions," he continued, referring back to his earlier comment, "because then we on the ship actually could have received directions from Amuro, riding point out there in his Gundam."

Sleggar leaned his body forward and practically thrust his large chin in Saila's face. She made as if to move away, but he ignored her. "Well, Saila," he said, "tell me . . . how'd you know the enemy was approaching?"

"Gee," she replied. "I didn't really 'see' them. It was sort of like there was a flare of reddish light inside my head." Turning to Mirai, she asked, "Isn't that the way it seemed to you, too?"

Mirai had taken her boots off and was relaxing in an almost disheveled pose on a sofa in the room. "It sure did," she said. "It was almost like seeing them, though. But that was just this one time. It's not always like that. Maybe the enemy *wanted* to make sure we spotted them today."

Kai glanced at Hayato and commented, "Beats me whatever these fair damsels are talking about."

"I bet it's sort of like the sparks you see when someone slugs you," his comrade replied.

Then Kai turned toward Amuro and said, "It's a sort of a white light, isn't it?"

Amuro loosened the collar of his uniform and said, "Maybe you guys were slugged by Lieutenant Ralv one too many times during training." Then he felt Saila's gaze on him and fell silent.

Mirai had sensed something different about Saila the moment she had entered the room. She knew Saila had been out the night before, but Amuro was the last person she would have imagined her with. Reflecting on it, though, she realized it was possible. Amuro had once had a crush on Saila, yet something in the way the two were acting with each other now suggested a much deeper bond. Was it, she wondered, some sort of New Type psychic affinity?

"I agree with Mirai," Amuro said. "I think the enemy deliberately wanted us to see the light. I felt some sort of weird psychic pressure directed at me, something telling me it was coming. We know the pilot of the Elmeth on *Texas* was a New Type, right? But there was something different about today." He was not being exactly honest. He had no intention of telling anyone—even Saila—exactly *how* different Lala Sun had been.

"What do you mean," Sleggar asked, "by 'psychic pressure'?"

"It was a menacing sensation," Amuro answered. "And it was projected right through the Mobile Armor fuselage. The sort of thing you might feel if a sworn enemy was standing right in front of you."

" 'Menacing,' eh?" Sleggar said with an awed look.

"Damn," Kai interjected, sounding almost jealous. "I never felt anything that specific."

"See?" Sleggar said, turning to Hayato. "Even if we had nine lives, we still wouldn't stand a chance against an enemy like that."

"I'll say," Hayato agreed.

"You know, what bothers me," Brite said, "is that if anyone told this story to the other pilots in the Force, they'd quit the next day."

The skipper was right, Amuro realized. It was the reason New Types weren't officially recognized in the Federation Forces yet and the reason their deployment in combat was still top secret. "You know what I think?" he said. "If New Types are really all they're cracked up to be, there oughta be a way to use them not just to wage war but to stop it."

"You must be out of your mind," Brite said. "It's hopeless as long as Zeon is under the thumb of the Zavi family."

"Besides, Amuro," Kai added. "Look at the Federation. The war'll never stop as long as the government brass, the Earth faction or Natives or whatever they call 'em, insist on controlling the space colonies from their 'home' planet."

That was more than Brite could let pass. He stood up and spoke slowly, caustically. "*Mister* Kai Shiden, we don't allow talk like that around here. And it doesn't seem befitting of a Federation officer involved in a holy crusade to defend our sacred Mother Earth."

"The skipper's right, Kai," Sleggar added with a grin. "You'd better be careful, 'cause for all you know I could be a spy sent by the Jaburo bureaucrats, and I might squeal on you."

There was something plausible about the way Sleggar said it, if for no other reason than the fact that there were murky aspects to his résumé. He had been bounced from unit to unit for bad conduct, but he was still stationed on the front lines of the war. And none of the core crew on the *Pegasus II* thought much of him, either. He had a reputation for being a womanizer and an officer incapable of controlling his troops, who were as undisciplined as he was.

"Who gives a damn?" Kai retorted. "The skirted Suits we let get away today are totally different from the old Zaks we're used to. And what about the new Mobile Armor we encountered that Amuro says sank one of our cruisers? Frankly, I don't care if you rat on me or not, Sleggar. I stand a lot better odds than you do of buying the farm out there in space."

Sleggar stopped leaning over Saila and stared at the floor for a second. It was clear that Kai had spoken for almost all the other core crew members. Everyone felt a new sense of danger.

"Tell me, Amuro," Sleggar asked softly, "what are those units that accompany the main Mobile Armor?"

"I don't know exactly," Amuro replied. "I've never been able to get a close look at them."

"Can you spot one close enough to shoot it down?"

"You're the gunnery officer. Have you ever tried shooting down a missile? It's like that."

"Hmm. I guess you'd just have to put up a defensive barrage and hope for the best."

"Imagine you're dealing with a conventional homing missile," Amuro explained, "but the thing is a heck of a lot faster and has an ability to slip up on you from your blind spot. And it's carrying a beam cannon."

"Wow." Sleggar looked over at Kai and said, "Well, in that case it evens the odds between us on the ship and you guys out in the Suits, doesn't it?"

Kai grinned, turned to Brite, and asked, "You got anything for us to drink, skipper?"

"Some New Type candidate you are," Brite retorted. "Find it yourself! And while you're at it, think of this as your last night on the moon. If we embark tomorrow on a new mission, we're headed straight for Zeon!"

Amuro looked at Saila when he heard Brite's words, but she avoided his glance and started walking away. It made him feel uneasy. He started to follow her, but as he passed Sleggar, the gunnery officer slapped him on the rear end and chortled, "Way to go, playboy!"

"I do something wrong, sir?" Amuro bantered.

"Nope, not a bit. Be my guest!" Sleggar replied, grinning.

It was a momentary interchange but enough to make everyone in the armory burst out laughing. When Saila, almost out the door, turned around and realized what was going on, even she blushed.

Brite, in an admonishing tone, said, "*Mister* Sleggar

Row, mind your manners, please. You'll be a bad influence on the lad.''

''Er, sorry, sir,'' Sleggar said. Since everyone had filed out of the room except himself, Brite, and Mirai, he turned to her and brazenly inquired, ''Well, ahem, in that case, what about you, mademoiselle? Free tonight?''

''Unfortunately for you, sir,'' she answered curtly, ''the answer is an emphatic *no*.''

Brite, ignoring the dialogue between the two, called up to the ship's bridge on the communications monitor. ''This is the skipper. I'm going to be down here in the armory another thirty minutes or so.''

Sleggar glanced quizzically at his superior and shrugged his shoulders. Then he finally stood up and left Brite and Mirai alone in the room, seated together on the sofa.

''Can you get some rest?'' Mirai asked Brite.

''Yeah. I'm off duty at one o'clock,'' he answered.

She made no attempt to leave. He looked at her and said nothing. He knew it might be their last chance to relax together like this.

''Is there something you wanted to tell me, skipper?'' she asked.

''No. I just wanted the chance to look at you a little. You don't mind, do you?''

''No, but it makes me feel a little embarrassed. You want to talk?''

''Not particularly. I'm a little worried about our mission, but there's nothing unusual about that. I just hope everything goes the way it's supposed to. I really appreciated the way the crew all gathered together here earlier. Something about it made me feel a little calmer.''

"Everybody's used to the way things work around here now."

Brite toyed with the idea of asking Mirai to sleep with him but never brought it up. It wouldn't seem right in their present situation, and the last thing he wanted to do was complicate things before they went into combat. Mirai clearly felt the same. A feeling of peace came over them. For several minutes they said nothing and merely enjoyed each other's presence.

Mirai hinted only once at the potential for intimacy. "Maybe when the campaign's over," she said, "we should put some pictures on the wall in this room. I'll buy some for you."

"A good idea," he replied. "It does look a little barren in here."

Saila and Amuro also found they needed few words. They embraced in silence, their young bodies craving each other, but Saila had a deep, unspoken regret, and Amuro knew what it was—the remark she had made earlier about killing her brother. But he didn't mention it, and neither did she. In the silence of their embrace they fully accepted and understood each other's differences, and not just because they were New Types.

Amuro stopped thinking about his childhood sweetheart, Fra Bow. And he realized that sometimes the hunches he experienced were wrong. And for some reason that made him feel good.

"Both you and your unit performed admirably, Commander," Krishia Zavi commented to Sha Aznable. "I must say that was quite a feat, destroying nine enemy ships in a matter of minutes. I understand Junior Grade Lieutenant Kusko Al was piloting the Elmeth."

Sha knew Krishia was pleased, but he also knew her position in the Zeon hierarchy was eroding. He had no idea what had happened in his absence, but she and her brother Gren, the supreme commander, were clearly on even worse terms than before. Perhaps, he thought, she had deliberately antagonized Gren by placing the New Type Corps under her direct control.

Krishia turned to the other officer in the room, Commander Garcia Dowal. "I want you to give top priority to locating more New Type candidates," she said. "Things are going so well, I might just make the New Type unit the centerpiece of our space attack forces."

Krishia's statement, Sha realized, was symbolic of a larger problem. She was a military leader who had once possessed considerable insight into problems of strategy and tactics, but now she was beginning to lose her perspective. The attack on the Federation's *LH* moon base had been a highly useful test of the New Type Corps. It had been important to use the unit in actual combat and assess its potential. But the most surprising discovery had actually been that the Federation's Gundam model Mobile Suit was apparently back in action and more powerful than ever. Sha had, in fact, been grateful that Lt. Sharia Bull was on his side. The man was a godsend, even if he was a spy sent by the Supreme Commander. He was mature and awesomely aware of everything around him, and the test sortie had proved he would stand firmly behind Sha as long as he understood his goals and deemed them worthy.

"Kusko Al," Krishia continued, addressing Sha again, "has proven quite a successful graduate of the Flanagan Agency, hasn't she?"

"Indeed she has, Excellency."

"And your future plans for her?"

"It's simple. We'll put her out in front in the Elmeth, and myself and the other Rik Dom pilots will support her. She's highly capable."

"Good! As long as you have faith in her, Commander, I'll leave the immediate combat decisions up to you. Our next mission starts in twenty-four hours. As you know, in some of our other operations the regular military hasn't done as well as they should have, and we can't leave everything up to them, which is why I'm asking you and your team to make an extra effort. You understand the situation, of course."

"Er . . . yes . . ." Sha was beginning to regret some of his own words. Krishia was Krishia. And perhaps because she was a woman, she was quite capable of seeing through his own plans. Women had that special way about them.

"I want you all to get some rest tonight," Krishia said. "From now on the New Type Corps—the 300th Autonomous—will be the center of our operations."

Sha knew there was an element of sarcasm in the way she had said "center of our operations." In the final master plan conceived by the Zeon forces and code-named Revol I, the *Abowaku* forces would be used as a decoy to draw out the Federation fleets so that Dozzle's forces from *Solomon* could destroy them. Krishia's warship, the *Swamel*, would then lure the surviving Federation Forces into position so they could be annihilated by the Solar Ray cannon being developed in the System project. There were still several hurdles to be overcome before the plan could be properly initiated, but Krishia's impatience was evidence that it would start soon.

Among the problems, the New Type Corps, while possessing a name, was still a fighting unit based on an as yet vague and unproven concept. If each member's unique abilities could be fully exploited in combat, the overall military gains might be enormous, but one Elmeth had been destroyed and the third had still not been delivered. The original plan had been for Sharia Bull to be the new Elmeth pilot, but the mechamen in charge of the project had refused. The psychom interface, they claimed, had already been specifically adjusted and set for Kusko Al.

Turning to Commander Garcia, Krishia asked anxiously, "We currently have six Rik Doms and only one Elmeth. What happened to the plans for reinforcements?" She had gained a great deal of confidence in her New Type unit and already wanted to strengthen it.

Her logic was simple: The greater the number of people and machines, the better.

"Excellency," Garcia replied, "it's a matter of what level of performance we want to maintain. We have about twenty potential candidates for the corps—"

"Why not enlist them all?" she demanded.

Sha interrupted. "Excellency. Allow me to be frank, but we should be careful here. The issue's not the *number* of pilots we have. Even at our current strength, if we just refine our teamwork, we can completely annihilate a large enemy force. The most important thing is to have experienced, seasoned pilots. For now I strongly recommend against a hasty increase in the unit."

"Hmm. I think I understand what you're trying to say, Commander, but it certainly should be possible to train other candidates in combat as part of a separate, detached force. But don't worry, I'm not asking *you* to undertake their training."

"Thank you for your consideration, Excellency," Sha answered. "I'll try to ready my own unit as fast as possible." He saluted, did an about-face, and started to leave. Krishia said something to Garcia on his way out, but he was not listening.

Outside the office door Krishia's secretary promptly rose to her feet and greeted him with an "Always pleased to see you, sir." Something about the way she said it surprised him and temporarily put his mind in a different mode.

He knew he had other business to attend to. Kusko Al, for example, was upset, and he had to help calm her down. But he said it, anyway. "You have plans for this evening?" he asked, his face mask glinting in the light.

* * *

All six Rik Dom pilots in Sha's unit had returned from the attack on *LH* with a kill to their name, and all were relieved because the new Suits had performed better than the old Zak model. And the members of the unit seemed to function superbly as a team. No one made snide asides about having such a young leader—they were all battle-seasoned veterans, perfectly capable of recognizing and appreciating Sha's skills as a leader and his remarkable ability to calmly appraise even the most desperate situation—his choice of route to attack the Federation *LH* moon base, for example, had seemed treacherous at first but had allowed their hit-and-run strategy to succeed. All of them, including Lt. Sharia Bull, had also been brought closer together by the mutual realization that they might have something *profound* in common—that they might be true New Types. The result was an unprecedented sense of solidarity and trust, a feeling that they could always depend on each other for aid during combat and that as long as they worked together as a team, as comrades in arms, they might avoid death in battle. It seemed almost as though they were connected by a thread of consciousness, as if instead of six individuals, they were a single unit with six sets of eyes watching out for the enemy. Although physically unable to see what the others observed, they knew how the team was moving and positioned, and when one team member felt the shock of sighting an enemy, the others could sense it, too. And when their Rik Doms returned to base and they looked up at each other's Suits, they felt a union of spirits. It was a good feeling.

There was only one qualifier to their sense of solidarity. It did not guarantee that the pilots liked each other as individuals outside the team context.

* * *

"Commander!" Sharia announced to Sha. "Kusko'll be all right. She's calmed down now. She's a pretty tough Wave." He grinned and started walking toward the briefing room.

"She's with Junior Grade Lieutenant Cramble, right?" Sha asked.

"Yessir."

"I think they're a little too similar in personality, don't you?"

"Maybe it's better that way if they have to work together. Sometimes Kusko's a little high-strung and strong-willed at the same time, and she has trouble controlling herself as a result."

"Think she'll work out?"

"She's certainly got the potential to."

Sha and Sharia entered the briefing room together and found Lt. (jg) Cramble refilling Kusko Al's coffee tube.

"You come here to make fun of me?" she asked.

"This isn't the time or place for that, Kusko," Sha said. "How do you feel?"

Cramble deferred to both Sha and Sharia, offering them a seat.

"Everyone's *so* considerate around here," Kusko said. The bitterness in her eyes told a different story.

"We're only being nice," Sha said, "because we're thinking of our own skins. Cramble here's probably the only one being nice out of pure altruism." He glanced at the man and then added, "We're worried about the *team*."

"Think you can sleep tonight?" Sharia added. "That's our concern now."

"I'm sorry about all this. I'm sure I'll be able to go

out again on a mission tomorrow. I swear I'll do my best."

"We heard you were having headaches and nausea and were worried. I know it's rough to work with the psychom interface."

"I'll be fine."

Cramble piped up from behind Kusko Al, "We rechecked the Elmeth system, sir."

During the fray in space with the Federation Forces, only Kusko's Elmeth had survived a hit from the Gundam. The beam had in fact been a near miss, but the diffused particles on its perimeter had caused more than minor localized damage. The blast, equivalent to a direct hit with conventional explosives, had momentarily knocked Kusko unconscious and had left her in a state of shock. She had never been hit before, and equally disturbing, she had been hit by a far-off marksman.

Until then she had easily detected the Federation ships deploying themselves around the *LH* moon base. They were far easier prey than the remote-controlled target ships she was used to practicing on; she could practically see curdling waves of fear emitted by terrified crews inside the metal hulls. But her basic temperament made her take combat too lightly. It allowed another flare of consciousness—a narrow thread—to infiltrate her mental space and allowed an enemy to snipe at her from afar. To her, the talk about a Federation New Type unit had been just that—talk—so that when the alien thought waves had come toward her, she had had no idea what was happening. No one had ever told her she might have to fight another New Type. Not even Sha. He had never fully comprehended the battle he had witnessed between Amuro and Lala on *Texas*, and even if he had, it was doubtful that he could have explained it to Kusko. New Type battles were far too new a military development.

If Kusko was too ignorant of New Types on the Federation side, she also had too much confidence in her own New Type potential. She had forgotten that people were often controlled by their immediate emotions but that there was a time lag between an emotional response and one based on rational thought.

Kusko handed her coffee tube back to Cramble. She looked at Sha and Sharia and said, "Guess I'm not as smart as I thought I was."

It was a spontaneous comment, but both Sha and Sharia knew it was spoken from the heart.

"Nobody's all-intelligent, Kusko," Sha said as if to console her. "That's why the teamwork's so important. Remember what we said earlier about being nice to you to save our own skins? That's what it's all about. About helping ourselves by helping the team. That's all it takes to make the team concept work."

"The commander's right, Kusko," Sharia added. "If you'd just reign yourself in a little, we'd all get along better and work together better. It's important not to overestimate yourself in this business. And by the way, the final maintenance check on the Elmeth is scheduled for tomorrow morning, so we need you to get some sleep. Let us know if you need any pills."

"Thanks, but I think I'm fine."

"Of course you are!" Sha responded deliberately with a smile.

Kusko removed a pin from her chestnut-colored hair, and in the weightless environment it fluffed, framing her face. Then she stood up, grabbed the nearest lift-grip, and left the briefing room area, her long, attractive legs flowing behind her.

Cramble turned to his two superiors and remarked with a smile, "Not a bad girl, eh?"

"She'll be useful in battle," Sha said, "but the Federation's rapidly acquiring the same capability. It's safe to assume their Gundam model Mobile Suit—probably piloted by Amuro Rey—is back in action. Don't forget that he's the one who destroyed Lala Sun. The leaps in ability that he's making suggest a powerful New Type."

Sharia added, "And don't overlook the Mobile Suits they're deploying around the Gundam, including the Gun Cannons and the GMs. They're formidable foes in their own right."

"The Elmeth is what gives us the advantage," Sha said. "Without it, we'd be exactly matched in strength. I just hope we can become the core fighting unit Her Excellency expects."

After taking off from *LH*, the *Pegasus II*'s unit gradually linked up with the main forces around the Federation's *FS* beachhead on the far side of the moon. Every conceivable type of supply and repair unit was involved in the operation in a supporting role. Even elite reinforcements from Luna II—the Federation's ace in the hole—joined the growing fleets, leaving almost no effective reserves in the entire Federation. Yet not a single ship in the vast armada had received concrete word of its final destination.

After a meeting on *FS*, Lt. Brite Noa returned by launch to the *Pegasus II* and summoned all pilots.

"Thanks for coming," he began. "Within eighteen hours our unit—the 127th Autonomous—will move from its present position toward Area 365, so all preparations must be completed by then. We'll be supported by two squadrons of Cosmo fighters, whose ETA is 2000 hours. At 2100 we'll have a joint operations strategy meeting with their pilots. That's it for now."

The MS pilots looked around at each other, knowing their time had finally arrived. Hayato Kobayashi had the honor of speaking for the rest.

"What's going on, skipper?" he said. "I know you can't tell us our target yet, 'cause you probably don't even know yourself, but the *Pegasus* is basically an MS landing craft. We're not designed as a full carrier for fighters."

Brite stepped up to the captain's seat on the boom crane in the middle of the bridge area and sat down. "How the hell should I know what's going on?" he said as he began to check the ship's internal communication system. "That's why I called you all here. Lieutenant Commander McVery of the 203rd Squadron is in charge of the Cosmo fighters. He's a veteran combat pilot, and I know he won't get in our way."

"I bet we're gonna attack *Abowaku*, right?" Kai said.

"Yeah," Hayato added. "I'll bet General Staff thinks we're a pretty easy group to get to do whatever they want."

"You think they're just using us?" Amuro asked.

"Yup," Kai answered.

"They just shift us around from one battlefield to another every week," Ensign Kria Maja, the GM 325 pilot, said as if supporting Kai.

"Sure seems that way," Kai added, making as if to

leave the room. "Damned if I understand what's going on. I wonder what the hell the general's thinking."

"Having us spearhead the attack, that's what," Amuro said. "Probably capture *Abowaku* and plunge into the Zeon heartland." He looked up at the ships in the Federation armada displayed on the ceiling screen above him and began counting. To the untrained eye the armada would have been more than adequate for the job, but the rules of modern warfare had changed.

Saila also glanced at Brite and asked, "Can't you at least tell us the code name of the operation, skipper?"

"Cembalo. It's an archaic type of musical instrument, sort of like a piano."

"What's that got to do with what we're going?"

"Probably nothing. Somebody in General Staff probably just liked it. Maybe it's like the time part of a poem was used as a code name in a campaign. I think it was the poet Paul Verlaine's line, 'With long sobs the violin-throbs of autumn wound my heart.' "

"When was that, sir?" Amuro asked, suddenly impressed with Brite's erudition.

"During an old global war in Europe if my memory serves me correctly."

Mirai glanced at Amuro but first addressed Brite. "There's something about all this that bothers me," she said. "When I read Amuro's combat report, it almost sounded like he's some sort of esper or something. I bet headquarters is relying on that and using all of us on the *Pegasus II* as a sort of secret weapon. What do you think, Amuro? Do you think if this war's ever over we'll be able to lead normal lives? Think New Types will really ever be accepted back in society?"

"You're jumping ahead too much, Mirai," Amuro answered. "Do you think we're true New Types? I'm still not sure we've done anything to really deserve that label.'' He leaned back against one of the windows on the bridge and glanced up at Brite in his perch. Having checked the ship's intercom system, the skipper was sipping coffee from the tube used in a weightless environment.

''Wait till the mass media get ahold of the idea,'' Brite said in between sips.

''But skipper,'' Amuro responded, ''nobody's really even come up with a precise definition of what a New Type is yet. It's too early to even think about how people will react to them.''

''Amuro,'' Saila said, ''don't forget what happened to Zeon Zum Daikun. He advocated the New Type concept and wound up being persecuted by the Earth Federation. And people knew a lot less about New Types then than they do today.''

Everyone on the bridge knew Saila was right, and Mirai replied for them. ''I'll say,'' she said. ''Just wait and see if the *Pegasus* survives this war. For sure Amuro'll be treated as an ace. A *New Type ace*. The mass media will love it. And for better or worse, New Types will be presented as something they're not.''

''Man with supernatural powers,'' Brite added, tongue in cheek. ''A telepath. I can see the headline already, saying, 'Lt. Commander Amuro, the Federation ace who can read your every thought!' ''

Brite said it as a joke, but Amuro knew he and Mirai were probably right. He tried to imagine how he would respond if it all ever came true but gave up. It was too depressing. But by the time Mirai's fears were realized, he and all the other core crew on the *Pegasus* would hopefully be a lot older and wiser and better able to deal with it. ''You surprise me, Mirai,'' he said. ''I always thought you were more of an optimist. I'm sure it'll work out."

"I hope so," she responded. "But something about it all bothers me. Saila . . . what do you think? I just can't help worrying."

"Maybe you're worrying too much," Saila replied. "You have been working awfully hard recently."

"Well, in that case," Mirai joked, turning to Brite, "maybe I could get a break after this meeting."

"I think we can arrange that," he answered curtly but with a grin.

"All right, Saila," Mirai said with a wink. "What do you say the two of us go out for a drink tonight?"

"Now, hold!" Brite said. "You're not serious, are you? There's no liquor on board! Is there?"

"Of course not, silly."

Amuro couldn't help but laugh at the way Mirai bantered with the skipper. "I'd love to join you both," he said to the two women.

"Enough out of you, *Mister* Amuro," Brite retorted. "You can go below immediately! There's a strict ship rule against private chitchat when on duty."

The captain was right, of course, but the idle talk was a welcome relief from the tensions building on board. And it was a reflection of a new camaraderie developing among the core crew, a closeness based on more than the mutual tolerance and affection that friendship normally implied, and supported by a growing New Type awareness. The crew had few chances to talk in terms that all understood and appreciated, but it was opportunities like these, however fragmentary, that they needed. Most were not yet evolved enough to create the extreme understanding and psychic harmony that

Amuro and Lala had experienced. They still needed more peak experiences of communication.

Sha Aznable sometimes felt the same way. And perhaps this was one of those moments. But he certainly had nothing that specific on his mind now. He was proud but not arrogant enough to give priority to such personal philosophical questions, not when he was lying next to Krishia Zavi's secretary for the first time.

"My real name's Margaret Ring Blair, Commander," she said with a smile. "And it's my *real* name."

Sha had a naturally suspicious mind, but with one sentence Margaret had managed to disarm it. She laughed, let her full-bodied hair fall over her face, and then looked up at him. "You look *awfully* scary," she said, not looking at all as if she meant it. She kept giggling as if she were somehow able to see through the serious facade of his life and even laugh at it.

There was something about her innocent mannerisms that he liked, something about the way she could see through people yet not offend them. He might even be able to fall in love with her, unfettered by the sort of savior complex he had had with Lala Sun. Deep down he was an extraordinary idealist. And because of his idealism he was normally incapable of totally trusting or loving any individual. Incapable of even making his only sister happy. Love, he believed, was an ideal. Love should be perfect and pure. Physical love, he believed, always condemned a man to remain at a physical level. In the case of Lala Sun, only his desire to "save" her had helped elevate his love to a higher plane.

"Does the, er, scar on my forehead bother you?" he asked. He was bemused by his own tongue-tied manner. Shyness was an aspect of himself that he could scarcely imagine in his normal military persona. He couldn't recall ever asking Lala Sun what he had just asked Margaret.

"Well, it *is* rather ugly," she replied bluntly. "Not a pleasant sight at all. But frankly I think it looks rather good on you, Commander. Forgive me for saying it," she hastened to add, "but I just wanted to be honest. It doesn't bother me. Really."

"Thanks," he replied. "You're being kind. You're everything I imagined when I first met you." He cursed himself for phrasing it that way. It seemed like that was the only sort of thing he was ever capable of saying. *I want to love her and tell her so,* he thought, *but I don't really know her well enough yet.* Perfectionism was a tragic shortcoming in his romantic character, one that always seemed to emerge at times like these.

He liked the way she interacted with him; he liked her sincerity and the way she didn't pressure him. She gave him such a sense of relief that all his senses—normally so taut—relaxed. As long as he felt her body next to his, it seemed there was nothing to worry about. *Who cares about New Types?* he thought, turning around as she moved slightly next to him. Her cheeks had a glow to them, and her full lips were formed into a smile. With his left hand he traced the lines of her full waist and suddenly, spontaneously wished she could bear his child. It was something he had never dreamed of with Lala Sun. Perhaps, it occurred to him, humans often acted on impulses like that, and then spent the rest of their lives trying to reconcile them with reality. There was something interesting about that idea, something to savor.

He could hardly remember what it was that had attracted him to Lala Sun and why he had tried so hard to look after her.

It was time to sleep.

Lieutenant Commander McVery's 203d Squadron with its twelve Tomahawk Cosmo fighters was stationed on the upper deck of the *Pegasus II*'s "leg" section. With the squadron and its support units, the *Pegasus* had finally taken on the organized hustle and bustle of an active warship. It was a new ambience that helped offset both the basic manpower shortage on the ship and the extremely informal atmosphere that existed among the original crew.

McVery, a dyed-in-the-wool space pilot, epitomized the change. He had the type of personality that had to be experienced to be fully understood: an informal manner that coexisted with a cautious approach bordering on nervous obsession. Wherever he was on board, he liked to yell out, *"This thing's not a warship! It's a den of disorder and poor training. I feel like I'm off to play war with a bunch of kindergarteners!"*

Sleggar Row and other *Pegasus* crew members often made cracks about McVery, saying that "he's riding awfully high on his hobbyhorse for a newcomer to the ship." McVery would then do an immediate about-face and always claim his willingness to defer to the *Pegasus* crew. And in the next breath, since the Mobile Suit unit had been ordered to form the Tomahawk Squad's rear guard, he would threaten to shoot down anyone who moved into his field of fire.

"Poor McVery," Kai liked to say with a laugh. "He's just upset 'cause he's stuck in the Cosmo fighter ranks and he'll be there forever."

Kai and the rest of the crew had a tendency to belittle

the ability of both McVery and his squadron, but in reality Cosmo fighters still played an important support role for warships. The crew took McVery more seriously when he remarked that no one would be likely to survive the coming mission.

They knew the 127th Autonomous—the *Pegasus*, the *Cypress*, and the *Greyden*—was headed for Area 365 and that it had been assigned such scant protection because that was all the Federation was willing to spare until the fleet reached its as yet unknown staging point for the Cembalo operation. Once in Area 365, they would have no contact with other ships in the armada. Area 365 formed one point of a triangle completed by Zeon's *Solomon* and *Abowaku* space fortresses. To venture into this area meant that the 127th was being used as a strategic sacrifice. Put more politely, it was a decoy or at best a feint for the larger Armada operation. They were, in other words, on their own.

McVery put it in his typically eloquent fashion: "The brass obviously have a hell of a lot of faith in this New Type stuff. I think me and my men were dealt a lousy hand when we were assigned here. But lemme tell ya, I won't be easy bait. I'll take out at least ten or twenty Zaks."

The 127th Autonomous left the sunlit moon behind it and sailed toward Area 365 at primary combat speed. Brite, the skipper of the *Pegasus II*, had a special operations file with information about their exact destination, but its lock was programmed not to open until twelve hours had elapsed.

Along the way, the Gundam, Gun Cannons, and GM 324 and GM 325, piloted by Ensigns Sarkus McGovern and Kria Maja, practiced flying in attack formation, accompanied by four Bowl machines from the other two warships. The exercises had no strategic value, but they helped keep the MS pilots in a state of readiness.

When Zeon's MS unit had attacked the Federation's *LH* moon base, few of the Federation pilots or crew members had even spotted the Elmeth and fewer yet had realized it was piloted by a true New Type. Some crewmen listening to friendly radio reports had detected a mysterious dissonant sound that had seemed to reverberate deep in their brains before the Elmeth had fired its first blast; but those like Saila, who had realized what the sound meant, were a rarity. Only Amuro had intuitively known the enemy was part of a New Type combat unit and deduced its true strength. And only he had understood that its destructive power exceeded that of Lala Sun. His main regret was that he had never confirmed the exact number of attacking Suits—they had simply been too powerful for him to worry about counting, and they had not been fooled for a minute by an attempt to divide their forces. When up against an enemy like that, he wondered if it was really fair to rely on Kai and Hayato in their Gun Cannons, but he was encouraged by their performance. They had increased the speed with which they could come to his support as well as the level of their teamwork. With them, he knew he wouldn't have to worry so much about being caught with his rear exposed. But he hoped he had acted correctly. He was plagued with doubt that he might have tried to maximize his own chances for survival at the expense of his friends.

His own desire to survive the war had suddenly been strengthened by knowing Saila intimately. It was odd, because the notion of fighting for the chance to sleep with a woman—even to "protect" her—somehow skewed whatever sense of ethics or propriety he felt should exist on the field of battle. He was still naive enough to believe that fighters should be inspired to risk their lives for more noble causes, such as overthrowing a dictator or preserving democracy. Yet somehow his experience with Lala Sun had hinted at an entirely different possibility. It was a possibility he believed existed in his new relationship with Saila, too. It transcended physical sexuality. Men and women. Women and men. Amuro was becoming aware of a potentially new world.

"Amuro Rey in G3! Ready for landing!"

"Go ahead, G3! But be careful!"

As he closed in on the *Pegasus II* after practice, Amuro saw Saila appear on his three-inch communications monitor, almost as if she were right there talking to him. Then he heard First Deck Petty Officer Callahan Slay giving directions vigorously. *"Two minutes on the horizontal axis! Correct to the right!"*

"Roger!" he called back, keeping a careful eye on the flight floor of the first deck looming up at him. He imagined Callahan watching wide-eyed, checking the Gundam's entry into the ship, probably reacting the same way others had when he had first piloted the Gundam on Side 7.

"I can't believe this."

Lieutenant Commander McVery's eyes flashed under his thick eyebrows when he first saw the sixteen-meter-tall Gundam Mobile Suit parked in front of the MS elevator.

Amuro removed his helmet, held it by his side, and

tried to change the subject. "It wasn't a very useful practice, sir," he said.

"I don't care what anyone says," McVery sputtered, "but that *thing* still looks like a giant toy robot to me. Landings and takeoffs must be hell, no?"

"Not particularly, sir," Amuro said, ignoring McVery's astonishment. "I was trained for Suits from the start."

From his reading of history, Amuro knew that at the beginning of the twentieth century, under the old calendar system, the battleship faction in many navies had often been unable to adjust when aircraft were first introduced. Similarly, as a seasoned veteran, McVery was probably still attached to the "good old days" when Cosmo fighters had been in their primacy. If he had a problem adjusting, it was understandable—the Mobile Suit concept had taken root only about five years earlier and had been proved feasible in combat only when Zeon's Zak model had been developed. It was no wonder he still saw them as giant toys.

Without waiting for Callahan to officially announce the safe return of the other Suits to ship, Amuro drank a bottle of liquid vitamins and floated up to the briefing room. Brite was already there, and the rest of the MS pilots slowly drifted in one after another. Then McVery entered with his Cosmo fighter pilots.

"What are they doing here?" Amuro whispered to his skipper.

"I wanted them to hear you give the debriefing," Brite announced. "You're the leader of our MS unit, and we may be involved in a joint operation with them."

Amuro didn't like the idea. He was still in the process of learning, and the idea of giving a presentation in front of Lieutenant Commander McVery and his men, all older combat veterans, would be like the pupil lecturing the teacher.

"Don't worry," McVery said with a grin. "We won't get in your way." He was chewing gum, and the noise irritated Amuro.

Like Amuro, Kai, Hayato, Sarkus, Kria, and the pilots of the four Bowls were young, and they were nervous with McVery present. Amuro opened his flight notebook and looked at it. Then he addressed his unit. "Based on what I saw during practice," he said, "in real combat you guys'd all be dead ducks. But we've gotta be confident of our ability as New Types. Older military people may put pressure on us to do things differently, but it's important to ignore them." When he said the last sentence, he looked McVery straight in the eye. Then he continued.

"You probably don't understand what I'm talking about, so let me explain. It's one thing to be aware of the physical conditions and environment you're operating in, but there's something important beyond that. Recognize, be aware of what you see, store it as knowledge, and remember there's a lot more out there to look out for. Your senses have got to be wide open, reading information from every direction to catch it. Sure, you need the instruments in your cockpit. But remember, you can't always rely on them. Mostly, you've got to ignore them because the enemy isn't gonna jump out at you from inside your instrument panel. He's gonna come at you from outside your Suit. The moment you forget this, he'll take you by surprise. Now, maybe what I'm saying sounds like a contradiction, but anyone who doesn't understand the logic behind it sure as hell isn't a New Type and probably isn't even qualified to be a regular pilot. Wouldn't you agree, Commander McVery, sir?''

The sudden question caught McVery by surprise, but he grinned and said, ''They'll never understand it that way. You're making it, how shall I say, a little too *conceptual*. For a lad like you teaching your peer group, you've got to make things more concrete, specific, down to earth. Understand?''

''Yessir,'' Amuro replied. Out of the corner of his eye he saw Saila enter the room, apparently off duty.

McVery continued. ''I think you're talking about something like the *ki*, or 'spirit,' that martial arts people refer to. You're saying we can detect this and we'd better not forget it, right?''

''Exactly, sir,'' Amuro replied. Then he continued. ''And when we face an enemy New Type unit, the *ki*, for lack of a better term, is transmitted in an even more clearly defined form. It's sort of a situational 'pressure' you can sense, an almost 'evil' force you can feel coming toward you. Being able to sense this in a way makes it easier to confront the enemy, but the problem is that he's faster than most normal opponents. Infinitely faster. Which means that there's only one way to respond, and that's by operating almost reflexively, by anticipating the enemy's moves in advance. Judging by everyone's performance today, though, you guys would all have been blasted to smithereens.''

''Even me?'' Kai asked with a quaver in his voice.

''Even you,'' Amuro said gently.

''What about me?'' Hayato next asked.

''Sorry.''

''You're being a little tough on us, aren't you?'' Hayato complained.

''Sorry, but the important thing is to figure out what

to do about it. Remember, I'm assuming a Zeon New Type unit attacked our *LH* base. As I mentioned yesterday, I think the pilot of the Elmeth Mobile Armor is a New type and even more advanced than the one I encountered on *Texas*. I say that because there was even more interference with radio transmissions around *LH* than we would normally find with Minovski particles. That's why some people claimed they actually 'heard' something inside their heads, and that's why it should be clear to everyone that we're talking about something utterly different from normal radio waves. Whoever or whatever was out there emitting those waves is our enemy."

Amuro knew he still wasn't explaining things very clearly, and it irritated him. He wasn't used to standing in front of people and lecturing. But while he was talking he thought of something totally different. During the confrontation with the Elmeth over *LH*, he had suspected its pilot was a highly evolved New Type whom he would face again soon. But he had sensed more than a simple desire to kill him; he had sensed something dark, brooding, and ominous directed at him, a personal hatred with an almost masculine edge. For that reason, perhaps, it hadn't occurred to him at the time that the pilot might again be a woman. Now, suddenly, for a reason he couldn't understand, he wondered if it might not have been Kusko Al. Perhaps everything was all a matter of fate. That notion had occurred to him once before when confronting Lala Sun. But the here and now transcended fate. He had to live in reality.

The presentation continued for over two hours, and when the discussion turned to close-quarter combat tactics, McVery and his men finally left the room. In parting, the lieutenant commander said, "We're obviously living in different worlds because, frankly, I can't understand this stuff. As far as I'm concerned, this Zeon New Type unit you're describing is still just a bunch of men in giant robots. And I don't intend to let them get me.''

Combat veterans tend to be conservative and to cling to whatever methods worked for them in the past. They see little merit in adopting other tactics. In warfare, if a new, unknown tactic is adopted and fails, there are no second chances.

As the other men left the room, Amuro questioned out loud, ''I wonder how many are really ready for what we're going to encounter?'' He loosened his pilot suit and sat down, wondering when on Earth the Federation would develop the perfect suit. His underwear was cold from his sweat, and even his socks were damp. His toes felt like they were swimming. Only Saila was still left in the briefing room.

''Amuro, as long as you're leading the MS team, I know things'll work out,'' she said as if to console him. She was still pondering something she deeply regretted, that she had ever mentioned killing Sha Aznable. Ever since leaving Side 7 she had felt a tension inside her, but during the short time she had spent with Amuro in his room the other night, it had left her. Perhaps, she worried, she had opened herself up to him too much. She had spoken impulsively and created a rift between them. If Amuro was a real New Type, she had thought he would have been able to deduce what she really meant and not dwell on the words themselves. But she knew she had made a mistake. She had been too naive. If anyone could really read another's mind, know his history, and know why he actually said something, that person would not be a New Type, he would be God.

New Types were distinguished by a superior intuition and their remarkable "hunches," but they were not mind readers in the true sense of the word. If anything, they were distinguished by a superior ability to read their *own* minds and understand information ordinary people might overlook. But if one could know one's own mind, would that extend to the spirit? If so, might it not be possible to extrapolate the truly universal aspects of oneself to others and through this "bridge" truly read another's mind? Unfortunately, such a feat would probably require that both parties be similar New Types. Saila and Amuro were fundamentally different.

"I grew up with a complex about my real family, Amuro," she said. "And sometimes I don't trust people." She knew he was probably too naive to understand what she was trying to say. But in order for him to expand and grow as a New Type, she felt it was important. She looked at him, unable to apologize or retract her statement about Sha. If she did, she knew he would probably feel attracted to her for all the wrong reasons.

Amuro, for his part, didn't press the matter. He was fiercely attracted to her, but on the eve of a major battle he wanted to keep his emotions in check. But it was hard.

He looked up at her with a tired expression and said, "Saila, can't you feel it?"

"Feel what?"

"When I was talking here a minute ago, I felt something. Sha's on his way. And so is Kusko Al. It was almost as though I could feel the weight of their presence."

"Weight?"

"It feels sort of like a wall of pressure, I guess, and it's spreading out toward the *Pegasus II.*"

Saila thought she finally understood what he was saying. The "weight" he had referred to *was* something spreading, menacing . . .

"I thought it was just the normal stress before battle, Amuro."

"No, it's more defined than that. This may sound crazy, but you know what I think? I think we've got to put a stop to this operation somehow. I know that alone won't stop the war. There'd still be thousands of people killed in other areas of the solar system. I can't stop the war myself, but I think somehow the strongest people, the best fighters, have to get together and destroy whoever's causing this war to drag on."

"Destroy them? You must be dreaming, Amuro."

"Maybe. But listen, Saila, let me ask you. Do you really think that your brother—Sha Aznable or Caspar Daikun or whatever his real name is—*likes* this war? I bet he doesn't."

"No . . . I'm sure you're right."

"He's got his own goals and dreams, right? He's older than me, and he's been around more. I'm sure he does."

"Well, maybe . . ."

"That's why he mustn't be killed. And as long as he isn't too self-righteous about what he's doing, we ought to cooperate with him."

"Cooperate? With my brother?"

"It's only an idea. But if he's the type of person I think he is, we should cooperate as New Types."

"But Amuro, the people you're talking about are the ones who are causing the war. Things aren't so simple. The Zavis aren't the only ones to blame. Nor is our crazy mixed-up Federation government. It's the whole system."

"I know, I know. That's why we've got to find a way to end the war as fast as possible. Then we can work to eliminate the root cause of it."

Saila knew Amuro was right about her brother. That was probably why Sha had always avoided confronting her directly when she tried to stop him.

"Amuro," she said. "I always wanted Caspar to be my brother. I never wanted him to be Sha Aznable."

"Listen, Saila, I don't know your brother at all, but as long as he's the Red Comet, he's the enemy, and if I meet him in combat, I have to fight him. I have to protect myself because I don't have any guarantee he feels the way I think he does. But there's something about him I kind of admire. And I think a lot of other men in the Force feel the same, too."

"That's just because you never had an older brother."

"Maybe. It's true I always wanted one."

Amuro's voice betrayed a trace of resentment. Saila was surprised at his emotion. It had never occurred to her how hard it must have been to be an only child.

"Sometimes I think it's easier being alone, Amuro," she said, suddenly feeling like a little girl. "It's a lot easier than having a brother you love and then losing him."

Amuro said nothing. He stood up and left, slamming the door behind him. *What should I do?* Saila thought. The room felt suddenly chilly. Monitors on the wall showed scenes of each launch deck. Everything was quiet. She knew it was dangerous to have illusions about what New Types could or could not do, yet she was seized by the desire to follow both Amuro and her brother no matter what happened.

CHAPTER 15
THE ATTACK

"Amuro Rey?"

Lt. (jg) Kusko Al was so shocked when she heard the name that she repeated it out loud.

"That's right," Sharia Bull said, looking at her curiously. "We have information that he's the same pilot who destroyed the first Elmeth model, and that he's headed in our direction."

Kusko suddenly felt naked, embarrassed before Sharia, but she feebly tried to respond to his unvoiced questions. "I . . . I've met him before," she confessed hesitatingly. "On Side 6. I . . . I never realized he was capable of anything like that. He seemed so young."

The instant she had heard Amuro's name, a clear image had popped into her mind. He was waiting for her in front of the Flanagan Agency with the nervous look of a youth with more on his mind than just a platonic meeting. And there was something she had found rather charming about that, so much so that she probably would have gone along with whatever he suggested. After all, she had helped rescue him when he had drifted near the *Kasetta III* in his escape pod, and she had even helped him destroy it later. It wasn't as if they were total strangers. She had intuitively liked him, and that made her feel good. Just as she had enjoyed the New Type aspect of his character, so, too, had she enjoyed the idea of getting to know him more intimately. It had been a mistake not to bring the escape capsule back to the Flanagan Agency for a thorough investigation, but she knew the Federation had no weapons system that could compare to the psychom, and, following that logic, she didn't see how the capsule could have been all that important. It was only one part of the new Mobile Suit. Besides, she liked Amuro.

She turned and asked her commander, Sha Aznable, "Did you have a chance to see how developed he was as a New Type?"

"No," he answered, fidgeting with the collar on his pilot suit. "But I can tell you this. During the attack on *LH*, we're almost positive your Elmeth was hit by a blast from Amuro Rey's Gundam."

Kusko Al couldn't help muttering to herself, "I don't like the idea of Amuro Rey in the Gundam." She was a woman with strong likes and dislikes, but it had never occurred to her that she might develop strong feelings for an officer in the Federation Forces. Especially since he had reddish hair. That was normally enough to make her want to laugh. But there was something about the way he had regained consciousness on the *Kasetta III* and instinctively dealt with the crew in such a cautious manner, something about the way he had been so curious about his environment. More than anything else, it was the realization that he was a sensitive person that first had made her like him. Then, when she had learned that he was smart, the sort who did what he said he would do, and had enormous strength of character, her positive first impression had escalated to another level. Federation troops might have burned her parents to death, but Amuro Rey was different, so she would forgive him for being with the enemy. That was the way her femininity asserted itself. *Perhaps*, she thought, *I can even contact him through the psychom interface and let him know that I'm piloting the Elmeth.*

What Kusko Al did not know was that her naive sentimentality would be first swallowed and then crushed by the overwhelming reality of war.

When the 127th Autonomous reached Area 365, it was observed by Zeon scouts from both *Solomon* and *Abowaku*, as the most advanced, exposed unit in the Federation armada.

On *Solomon*, Dozzle Zavi told his men, "Ignore it. It's just a feint. Revil bypassed us to take *Granada* before. So now he's coming to get us. Get our forces out in position and keep them together."

General Revil, meanwhile, hoped Krishia Zavi would overestimate the importance of the 127th so that he could flush her *Abowaku*-based New Type unit out in the open. "After the fight on *Texas*," he commented to his staff, "Krishia will suspect we have our *own* New Type corps. It doesn't matter if the *Pegasus II* is really manned by true New Types or not. The important thing is that she *believe* the 127th is a true New Type unit."

"Do *you* believe it, sir?" an aide asked.

"It depends on their performance in battles to come," he replied. "At this point they look pretty good."

General Revil personally commanded the main Federation fleet centered on his flagship, the *Drog*, and the carrier *Trafalgar*, yet his fleet was only part of a giant armada of over 320 Federation ships. After leaving the moon, the armada had appeared positioned to strike *Abowaku* directly, but in actual fact neither the Zeon forces nor the crews of the Federation ships themselves knew where they would finally converge, for the armada was dispersed not just along a single plane but within a three-dimensional spherical area over ten thousand kilometers in diameter, nearly the same size as the planet Earth. In this vast space, 320 ships were like floating specks of dust in a cavernous hall, so dispersed that they presented little immediate military threat. But when collected together at their final rendezvous point, they would constitute an awesome destructive force. Mankind was standing on the brink of yet another bloody power struggle.

A single red light suddenly winked on the ceiling display over the *Pegasus II* bridge, and Ensign Mark Kran yelled, "Enemy ships sighted!"

The order immediately went out: *"Launch Tomahawk Squadron!"* The twelve Cosmo fighters under Lt. Commander McVery's command were released from their moorings and floated off the *Pegasus II* upper deck. With verniers deployed on a winglike design, they resembled fat spears. Referred to as "fighters," they had far greater firepower than did old-style heavy bombers.

The first Zeon force encountered was not a New Type unit but a special task force of three *Musai*-class cruisers from *Solomon*, carrying a total of six Zaks. Twelve rockets streaked from the cruisers toward the *Pegasus II*. Then five of the Zaks launched.

On the *Pegasus*, Brite issued a series of commands:

"They've penetrated the second combat line! Ready main cannon! Missile elevation zero point three degrees! Launch nine! Two volleys!" From twelve missile tubes on either leg of the ship's front section, two volleys of nine missiles each instantly streaked forth, leaving a trail of light among the stars.

"Initiate evasive action! B formation!"

"B formation!" Mirai yelled in response, flicking a switch on the panel in front of her, putting the ship on autopilot. If she had to maneuver quickly to evade an incoming missile or an attacking Suit, she could manually override auto, but as soon as the maneuver ended, the guidance system would default back to auto and thus keep the ship in formation. The warships following the *Pegasus*, the *Cypress* and the *Greyden*, began crisscrossing back and forth around her in an evasive maneuver, preparing for enemy missiles.

"Incoming at twelve o'clock, two minutes!"

From the bridge of the *Pegasus II* the crew suddenly spotted two bands of light from missiles streaking toward them, but in almost the same instant they exploded. A Federation Suit had picked them off.

"I think it was Amuro," Saila said softly.

"Lower protective shutters!" Brite yelled.

Shutters immediately descended over all the windows on the bridge, but the crew members never lost their view, for the inside of the windows now functioned as a display monitor.

"Second wave incoming!" Mark Kran, the operator, called out in a tense voice as he spotted a dozen streaks of light from approaching missiles.

"Ready ship guns!" Brite barked. "Fire at will! Fore missiles, raise vertical elevation point six degrees. Launch three volleys of twelve missiles each!"

It was the sort of missile defense that was nearly futile in three-dimensional space. The *Pegasus*'s anti-missile missiles streaked forth in what looked like a single band of light, but some of them appeared to have launched too close together and collided with each other, for mushrooms of light appeared not too far from the ship. Luckily, the incoming missiles were no more successful.

In telescopic mode, one of Brite's displays showed the three enemy ships among the stars, and he knew they were close enough for his main cannon.

"Target in range! Fire main cannon!"

Brilliant beams of light far more dense than the earlier missiles suddenly belched forth from the *Pegasus*'s two mega-particle cannons and pierced the blackness, stretching for what seemed like an eternity. They emitted sparks on their periphery, probably from contact with comet fragments or "star dust," but neither appeared to hit the enemy. It had long been rumored in the Federation Forces that Zeon's *Musai*-class cruisers were adept at evasion, and the difficulty the *Pegasus* had hitting them confirmed it. Twenty seconds after the *Pegasus*'s cannons fired, beams from the Zeon forces streaked back in retaliation, suggesting that they had a less sophisticated telescope mode on their gunsights and thus took longer to aim.

"Tough luck about the lousy optics," Brite yelled at the Zeon ships on the display monitor in front of him. "Just try and hit us!"

And then it happened. One of the beams from the *Pegasus* struck the left *Musai*, and an enormous burst of light flared in the darkness. But the explosion did not appear to have been fatal.

"Give the left one two more blasts!" Brite barked.

"McVery's squadron'll be there in five more seconds." He knew that from then on it would be too dangerous to support McVery with either beam cannon or missiles. And he also knew that the enemy Suits would soon be on top of the *Pegasus II*. It was critical that Amuro and his men destroy them before they could inflict any damage.

In the distance he spotted the telltale fatal mushroom of light from the left *Musai*.

"One *Musai*-class cruiser destroyed, sir!" Oscar yelled. "But I'm picking up what looks like a Zak at eleven o'clock, three minutes!"

Brite prayed Amuro's unit would intercept the enemy Suit. If the Zak followed normal Zeon tactics, it would try to slip under the ship's defenses. One never knew what would happen in a combat situation, but he had faith in Amuro.

The *Pegasus II* and the other three ships in the 127th group continued to close in on the enemy. When it appeared that Lt. Commander McVery had finally reached the *Musai* ships and commenced his attack, Brite could not help thinking, *I wish he had more than twelve fighters*. No matter how seasoned a warrior McVery might be, the odds against him were steep.

Amuro and his men steadfastly approached the five enemy Zaks.

"Give 'em hell!" he yelled into his mike, knowing that with the Minovski concentration they were encountering, it was probably his last radio transmission for a while. "And don't forget we're better than they are!"

Ensigns Sarkus and Kria had both been in combat before, but they had originally trained on Cosmo fighters, and the new GM Suits were harder to handle. The

GM's electronic 360-degree display system, for example, was nice but initially unnerving to a pilot used to direct visual sightings through a fighter's Plexiglas canopy.

Then the Zaks arrived. Sarkus met the first one, which unfortunately had the colored antennalike rod of a squad leader. He fired his beam rifle. The Zak easily evaded it and closed in. Sarkus yelled in terror, but in the same instant a beam pierced the Zak and it vanished in a ball of light. Amuro's Gundam had slipped up on Sarkus' right side.

"Sarkus!" Amuro barked into his mike. "Don't just fly with inertia! Move!"

"Ye-yessir!" the GM pilot responded.

Sarkus's GM was nimbler than a Cosmo fighter, and he tried to operate it as confidently as possible, flying in a zigzag pattern above the assumed line of combat. Then he heard Amuro's voice call out again, *"Ten o'clock, up fifteen degrees!"* Sarkus looked up and spotted the glowing mono-eye of a Zak. In rapid succession, several blasts creased his GM's armor. Cursing, panicking, he got the Zak in his sights and fired a volley from his beam rifle. With a *whoosh*, one blast hit home. The Zak began spewing beads of light from its back and then raised both hands as if clawing in desperation at the heavens. Then another beam hit home. The Zak's limbs disintegrated, and the entire Suit turned into a ball of light.

Then he heard, *"Sarkus! Don't waste your energy!"* It was the scolding voice of his unit leader—Amuro—again.

After Amuro, Sarkus, Kai, and Hayato had each made one kill, the entire MS unit chased the remaining Zeon Zak as it tried to flee back to its mother ship.

"Kria!" Amuro commanded. "I want you out in front!" He wanted to present the ensign with an easy target and let him aim at the retreating Zak, but the man somehow managed to bungle it and took two shots.

By the time the unit caught up with McVery's Tomahawk Squadron, the last remaining *Musai* had been badly damaged but was still putting up fierce resistance. Since McVery had already lost four of his fighters, Amuro's unit helped him out by slamming several beam blasts into the ship's prow and finishing her off.

Only thirteen minutes had elapsed between the moment of initial contact with the Zeon task force and its annihilation. In terms of firepower the *Pegasus II* and its accompanying ships had a slight advantage over the Zeon squadron, but in reality the battle had been determined by the effective tactics employed. Not a single attacking Zak had been able to penetrate the 127th's defense.

Back in the briefing room of the *Pegasus II*, Amuro stated his opinion emphatically. "That was nothing. They haven't even arrived yet. And I don't mean Krishia or Dozzle's regular forces. I mean Zeon's true New Type unit."

Lieutenant Commander McVery was still preoccupied with the last battle and could not resist a dig at Amuro's MS unit. "If you'd reached us earlier, *Mister Amuro*," he caustically commented, "I wouldn't have lost four of my fighters!" He knew that the criticism was not fair and that he was just saying it to let off steam. In reality he had been amazed at the speed with which Amuro and his men had joined the fray. He had heard that MS battles were essentially chase-and-be-chased melees, but in the entire war he had never witnessed such a feat. Five enemy Zaks had been unable to sink a single Federation ship and had instead been annihilated themselves. The 127th had achieved a phenomenal victory, but on a personal, emotional level he could not ignore the fact that several of his own men had been lost.

"Next time maybe we should form the rear guard," he joked lamely. He still had enormous pride in the vanguard role of his Cosmo fighter unit, and he was not ready for the answer he received.

Amuro took his words literally. "If that's what you'd prefer," he said, "we can try it next time, sir."

"Whoa, wait a minute, sonny," McVery answered in a quick about-face. "Let's be serious here. I'm a *Tomahawk* man. That's not funny."

"Well, sir, we'll eventually be confronting the same Zeon New Type Unit that attacked our *LH* moon base. Frankly, I don't think there's any reason for you to do anything suicidal. The most important thing, it seems to me, sir, is to defend the *Pegasus*. Don't you agree?"

"What are you talking about? Hell, the Red Comet or whatever he's called isn't some sort of supernatural character. Just because he can destroy a few Federation ships doesn't mean he can destroy the Tomahawk Squadron!"

"I'm sorry to differ with you, sir. But the unit on its way is far more powerful than the old Red Comet."

"You're talking about that Elmeth thing, right? Who knows what the hell these Mobile Armor contraptions really are, anyway. Right now we're just dealing with prototypes, right?"

"Perhaps," Amuro replied, standing his ground.

"No offense intended, sir, but in the interest of saving as many of your men's lives as possible, sir, I honestly think it would be better if your squad did take the rear."

The 127th Autonomous continued along its assigned course, but a turning point had been reached. General Revil's flagship, the *Drog*, fired off a blue signal flare that was observed far off on the Federation's *FS* moon base. *FS* then transmitted a coded laser message to each of the Federation fleets in the armada—*Proceed at third combat speed!* Each unit commander thus finally was permitted to open the secret file that had been delivered on departure and learn the armada's true target—Zeon's space fortress *Abowaku*.

Brite Noa, for his part, finally learned the 127th's true mission: to use all means available to destroy Zeon reinforcements from *Solomon*. He knew that the *Solomon* forces would not sit idly by during the ten hours in which the dozen or more Federation fleets formed a virtual wall between *Solomon* and *Abowaku*, and that if the armada were not careful, it would be constantly harassed from the rear by *Solomon* forces as it closed in on *Abowaku*. The 127th, at the highest elevation relative to the plane of the ecliptic, would act as a shield for the armada. And it would be the first unit attacked.

"Here we are," Brite grumbled from his captain's seat on the bridge, "the decoy, the bait, the sitting duck. If I understand this right, it looks like Revil's ships take on the main force from *Abowaku* while we hold off everyone else from *Solomon*."

"But that at least means the Red Comet won't come after us, right?" Kai seemed relieved when he said it.

"He's right, isn't he?" Amuro asked, glancing at Mirai.

Mirai pondered a minute. "I don't think so. We've won enough skirmishes to attract attention from all over. We'll be targeted by both *Solomon* and *Abowaku* forces, but since we're too small a unit for them to waste a large fleet on, I'll bet the special unit led by the Red Comet *will* eventually come after us."

Saila, manning the communications console on the bridge, removed her headset to better hear the conversation taking place around her. Could her brother really be coming toward them? Mirai seemed to think so. She felt trapped in a web of fate. In her heart she knew he was on his way.

On Vice Admiral Dozzle's flagship, the *Gandow*, the communications experts quickly noted the increased activity of the Federation Forces and the fact that they appeared to be converging around a single area in space.

"Don't they regard *Solomon* as a worthy enemy?" Dozzle wondered out loud. He felt oddly slighted by General Revil. But when he heard the news that three of his *Musai*-class ships had just been destroyed in a fray with a Federation unit, he was enraged.

"*What?*" he yelled. "They annihilated our cruisers in only ten minutes?"

"Er . . . yessir," a nervous junior officer replied. "One of our patrol ships in Field 550 sighted the explosions and went straight to the area, but it was too late. Our ships had already vanished, sir."

"Even though they had Zaks protecting them?"

"Yessir . . . six of them, sir."

"That should've been plenty! What the hell went wrong?" Dozzle's face went beet-red with anger, and he had to restrain himself from striking the officer giving the report.

"The Federation Force appears to be centered around a White Base–class ship, sir. We understand there may be a New Type unit involved."

"Who says so?"

"The skipper of the patrol ship, sir, Number 600."

Dozzle slowly lowered himself into a chair and commanded an orderly next to him to bring him some coffee. "Well," he said, "we certainly don't need the captain of some little patrol ship to engage in speculation, do we? That won't do when we're trying to formulate a coherent strategy. Our main battle isn't going to be with some fuzzy New Type unit or whatever it's called. I want our observation of the entire Federation armada beefed up. I want to know what route of attack Revil's going to take to *Abowaku*. We'll leave behind the minimum number of ships needed to defend *Solomon*. All others will launch with us."

After Dozzle barked out his orders, he reached out for his coffee tube and took a sip. "Just wait, Revil," he muttered. "I'll teach you a lesson you won't forget."

On *Abowaku*, Krishia Zavi couldn't help smiling when she heard of the change in the Federation movements. Technically speaking, she wasn't responsible for *Abowaku*. It was under her brother Gren Zavi's jurisdiction, and she was merely using it temporarily.

"Gren should fly here and defend the place himself," she snapped.

But could he arrive in time? It would still take several days before the System project could be completed. The real question was whether her own forces on *Abowaku* should move out to strike the Federation armada. And if so, with her limited strength, how should she inflict maximum damage on them?

"There won't be time for us to try and wipe out the Federation units one by one," Sha Aznable said. "We should wait until they come closer and converge."

"Why do you say that?" Krishia asked, noting that his view was at odds with the strategy put forth by the Zeon General Staff.

"Because the forces coming at us aren't omnipotent. We should draw them in closer and then crush them right in front of *Abowaku*. And I think Your Excellency's forces should lead the attack. If we try and hit their fleets individually, we might accidentally disperse them. That might gain time for the System project to be completed, but it would indirectly aid your brother, the supreme commander."

"I won't let him use the System. I'm going to show him what we can do without it."

"Your brother's an extremely ambitious man, Excellency. Remember, this is war. But I understand your wishes. I'll take my unit out to meet the enemy and hope Vice Admiral Dozzle comes through to help us."

Sha turned and started to exit Krishia's office. He felt angry. He wanted to tell her that in order to survive politically they should abandon *Abowaku* and flee. But he did not. He knew she was obsessed with the idea of staying and destroying the New Type unit on the Federation's White Base–class warship.

Margaret Ring Blair was standing and waiting nervously for him outside Krishia's office door.

"Are you taking off?" she queried.

"It looks that way," he said. "I think this is it. Take care of yourself, Margaret."

"Thank . . . thank you, Commander."

There were other secretaries and aides watching in the reception area, so he touched her elbow and gently motioned for her to accompany him outside. She immediately sensed his meaning and moved to open the door for him. Once outside, he turned to her.

"At this point, Margaret," he said, "the most important thing is to survive. Don't do anything rash. It's better to be a coward in this business. Look out for yourself."

"But . ." She started to say something but stopped.

"Don't worry about me," he said, placing his lips on hers. "I'll come back alive."

The rounded shape of the space attack ship *Madagascar* lay at rest on the darkened flight deck of *Abowaku*, ready for launch. The Mobile Suits and the Elmeth in Commander Sha Aznable's New Type unit had already been loaded.

"Well," Lt. Sharia Bull said, turning to Sha and grinning. "Where do we rendezvous with our Federation date?"

"The enemy *White Base* ship's apparently in Field 660. We don't know where one other ship in the unit is, but we'll aim for Field 600."

"Why?" Lt. (jg) Kusko Al asked.

"Because that's where the Gundam apparently sank a *Musai* cruiser," Sha said.

"Was Amuro Rey the pilot?"

Sharia laughed. What had once seemed a game to Kusko Al was clearly turning very real. "Who cares what his name is, Kusko?" he asked.

"I don't know. It just seems a shame to kill him. He wasn't a bad kid."

To Sharia, her attitude smacked of sentimentality, and he decided to rectify it. "Well, don't let your own abilities go to your head," he said. "Judging from what the commander has said, the 'kid' is a crack MS pilot, and there's a strong possibility he may kill us instead of the other way around."

Kusko was taken aback. She knew Sharia was right, but she had a competitive streak in her. She had been raised to ignore the differences between men and women, and she believed people should be judged on the basis of talent and ability, not gender. But war tended to wreak havoc with everything. And that was another reason she hated it.

"It's not like you to be so sentimental, Kusko," Sharia continued. "You, of all people, should have a healthy respect for New Type abilities. After all, you're the one this Amuro Rey character nearly managed to vaporize earlier, right?"

Sha and Sharia left for the *Madagascar*'s bridge, and Lt. (jg) Cramble came over to console Kusko. She tried to avoid him by climbing in the cockpit of the Elmeth, but he called out after her, "Don't take it to heart. Sharia's just being a little pompous. He's just trying to show himself off as a New Type."

"Thanks, Cramble. But don't worry. I'm okay."

She didn't think much of Cramble, and she never could understand why he fancied himself a ladies' man. To her he was just another oversexed male. As for herself, she knew she attracted men, but she was not going to exploit that; she believed she had a responsibility to improve whatever talents God had given her. She knew she had some, and she was proud of it. And Amuro Rey? His naivete clearly came from his youth. That she had liked him showed she was a woman, and as far as she was concerned there was nothing wrong with that. She also liked the fact that he had been broad-minded enough to have been attracted to a woman like herself.

But in battle she knew that she would meet an entirely different Amuro Rey, that combat might drastically transform his otherwise innocent personality. This in turn allowed her to realize that Amuro indeed probably *had* been the one who had nearly killed her. And from there her own acute intellect quickly led her to a conclusion: *I liked you, Amuro. But I have to kill you.*

Shortly thereafter, the *Madagascar* took off from *Abowaku*, supported by two Gattle fighter-bomber squadrons.

In the meantime, on the Federation side, the 127th Autonomous had detected a second enemy force approaching. It was no surprise. The officers on the bridge of the *Pegasus II* had known they would run into more and more resistance the closer they got to the heart of Zeon territory.

"It's been only six hours since the last attack, right?" Amuro said. The shapes of six or seven enemy ships had already been observed twenty-five degrees below the ship's starboard wing.

"Know what I think?" Lt. Commander McVery said. "I think there's finally been enough killing. When the whole campaign's over, the whole god-awful war's finally gonna be over, too." Then he laughed and added, "But this time my men and I'll form your vanguard again, Mister Amuro!" and hurried out of the room.

Amuro glanced up at Brite in the captain's seat above

him on the bridge. "Is McVery becoming a philosopher or what, sir?"

"Well," Brite replied. "Over five billion people have died in the war, and that puts a little brake on the population explosion. It's just McVery's backhanded way of saying that mankind may yet manage to overcome the biggest crisis of all time."

"Are you trying to say this war's just another form of population control?"

Brite looked at Amuro with an amused expression. "That's one way of looking at it," he said.

Unable to believe his skipper's words, Amuro let his anger show. "You've gotta be kidding, sir. That's not what I'm fighting for."

"You wanna stop?"

There was no way to respond properly. Amuro just stared back at Brite.

Mirai answered instead, coolly, saying, "While you're both debating, the enemy's on his way here to kill us."

"But Mirai," Amuro said, his anguished voice rising in volume, "I don't care if the skipper's joking. I think that sort of talk's an insult to all the people who've given their lives in the war. Don't you? We're not living in a video game world, are we? How many points to kill another human? One? Two? How many points was Lala Sun worth?"

Brite signaled Saila. Quickly reading his meaning, she stood up from her seat in front of the communications console and walked over to Amuro. Taking him by the arm, she said, "Amuro, you've got to calm down." Their bodies swayed in the weightlessness, but they both reached out and grabbed a fixture and pushed against it.

As they floated out the bridge exit, she said, "You don't really believe they're serious about people killing each other for such a crazy reason, do you? Just think, by building the space colonies we created room for billions more people to live. And life on the colonies has now stabilized. History can't go backward."

"I don't know, Saila. There *was* a weird logic behind what Brite said. It's based on the idea that man's fundamentally rooted to the planet Earth and that his population should be tied to it, too.

"But New Types are supposed to transcend all that, right? They're not bound by archaic ways of thinking and don't need to kill each other because of it, right?"

Amuro headed for the flight deck, and Saila followed him. When they boarded the flight deck elevator, they were at last alone. She suddenly turned and kissed him.

"Amuro," she whispered. "Unless we somehow stop this war, New Types'll never really come into their own. You've got to fight in order to end it. If someone like you dies, the old ways of thinking are going to last forever."

"You mean we've got to win over the 'Old Types,' right?"

"Over the land-based faction. The Earth faction. The Natives. Whatever you want to call them. New Types have to win over the people who don't realize that this war has become a habit, a collusion on a grand scale. I know what I'm saying's even more difficult than winning the war we're in, but New Types are going to have to *fight* for a world without war."

"Listen, Saila. Do you think your father really believed what you're saying now?"

"He never specifically told me this stuff, and I

wouldn't have been old enough to really understand if he had. But I know our world's changing, Amuro."

"What you really mean is that *we* have to change it, right?"

"Right. I don't know anything about Lala Sun, but maybe she was related to it all. Maybe New Types can transcend normal empathy among humans, even normal modes of human communication, but they're still human. You follow me?"

"I know. New Types aren't espers. I know *I'm* just an ordinary human. If there's any difference between me and people on Earth, it's—how should I say it?—it's that the light of the stars is just as important to me as the air is to them. For people to understand each other in a universe as vast as this one, we're going to need a lot more intuition and insight and a hell of a lot more patience."

"We need those qualities all the time, but in space they're critical, aren't they?"

"But most people are still locked into old ways of thinking and don't understand that yet."

Saila suddenly looked at him, smiled, and said, "You know, Amuro Rey, I think you're just the man to teach them."

He looked her in the eye and smiled, too. "Saila . . . pretty Saila. Thanks. Tell you what. I'll launch from the *Pegasus* and go fight today. Not for some high ideal. But for you. To protect you. How's that?"

She giggled. "Words like those make me glad I was born a woman, Amuro. They seem a little *too* romantic, but I'm not complaining. Go out and do your best. For me if you want. And when you come back let's talk some more about what we can do."

Saying, "Let me kiss you again," he bent his head and gently placed his lips on hers.

The second Zeon task force sent to destroy the 127th Autonomous consisted of two *Chibe*-class heavy cruisers, four *Salamis*-class regular cruisers, three Zaks, and one squadron of Jiko attack ships (resembling small torpedo boats). Although the 127th was outclassed in numbers and strength, McVery and Amuro's units lured the enemy into a defined combat zone and annihilated them. Incredibly, the entire action took less than fifteen minutes.

Two of McVery's Tomahawks were heavily damaged, but much to his relief, Hayato and Kria managed to rescue the pilots with their Mobile Suits. "In times like this," he later admitted, laughing loudly, "I guess those damned robot arms come in pretty handy, after all! And as for you, *Mister* Amuro Rey, well, let me congratulate you on the fine job you did training your men. From now on, lad, we'll work together like hand and glove!"

After returning to the *Pegasus* bridge, Amuro saw Saila. They winked and jokingly flashed the V for victory sign at each other. They did not know that with every victory the 127th was attracting an ever more powerful enemy.

"We're dealing with some full-blown New Types here," Sha Aznable said after demanding more speed from the *Madagascar*. "They're steadily increasing their performance and level of aggression."

With the Minovski level rising and radio transmissions no longer practical, laser communications were the only means the *Madagascar* had left to track the Federation fleet movements, and even lasers required predicting in advance approximately where the target was going to be.

"It's going to be hard to find them," Sha said, "but we've got to. If we don't stop them, the archduchy's entire line of defense will be compromised."

"I know you're right, sir," the *Madagascar*'s captain said. "But you don't really believe," he added with what sounded like a groan, "it's the same unit that wiped out our two task forces, do you?"

"Who else could it be? We're better off assuming the worst. That way, if we survive, we can break out the liquor and celebrate. By the way, any shoal regions ahead?"

"Only one, sir. Corregidor."

"Does it cover a wide area?"

"Yessir. Looks that way."

"Good," Sha replied, turning to leave the bridge area. "We'll try and ambush them there."

Now things get serious, he thought. He was both tense and exhilarated thinking about what his unit faced. Normally he just wanted to survive the war, but this time he knew he had more at stake.

Later, in the *Madagascar*'s briefing room, Sha privately addressed the MS pilots in his unit.

"Times are changing," he began. "I first began to believe in the New Type theory because of the Gundam pilot. And I now know New Types aren't just a mutant form of humanity. Nor are they just a weapon. Let me confess to all of you right now—and to hell with my own personal goals in all of this—I think we're on the brink of a era, a New Type era. And because of that, it's important that none of you be killed! Understand? The Earth Federation has formed their own New Type unit to use as a weapon against us. We will annihilate them. But beyond that, I want you all to refrain from senseless killing. Concentrate on destroying the weapons of war and not the people. Too many people have already been slaughtered, and we need to end the war, not prolong it. I want you all to go out there and fight bravely but stay cool and keep your wits about you at all times."

Kusko Al was moved by Sha's last words. She vowed she would use whatever powers she had to their fullest extent. That was simply the way she was. As the pilots all headed toward their Mobile Suits, she donned her helmet and thought to herself, *Amuro, if I run into you, I'll have to kill you, because by the time you realize who I am, it'll be too late—you won't be able to stop fighting. It's too bad, but that's the way war is.* She climbed into the Elmeth cockpit and frowned, for she knew her thoughts were only a means of covering up the growing nervousness she felt before combat. It was true that if it weren't for the war, she would never have met Amuro Rey. But she had no time to think of that. With a growing sense of rage, all she could think of was that if it weren't for the war, she would never have been placed in such a wretched position.

The *Madagascar* entered the Corregidor shoal zone, and while its Gattle fighter-bombers took cover behind the huge rock fragments in the area, the seven new Rik Dom Suits in Sha's unit deployed themselves with the Elmeth in the lead.

Sha's red Suit came up alongside Kusko's Elmeth and plunged ahead together with it. Sharia Bull's Rik Dom formed the rear guard. If the Bit units remotely controlled by the Elmeth could just destroy the Federation Horse, their work would be half over.

"Kusko!" Sha called. "Do you read me?"

"Loud and clear, Commander," she answered.

"The enemy'll direct cannon fire and missiles at us before we visually sight them. Don't just rely on your intuition to evade them at first. Follow me until you get the hang of things. Then, when we catch up with the warships, they're all yours. Sharia, myself, and the other Rik Dom pilots'll take care of the enemy Suits."

"Understood, sir," Kusko answered.

CHAPTER 16 THE ELMETH

Luna II continued circling Earth in its orbit 180 degrees opposite that of the moon. In addition to functioning as a Federation fortress, the former asteroid now also housed several thousand civilian refugees from colonies, most of whom had been mobilized to work for the various supply units or local military factories. Among them was Fra Bow, Amuro Rey's former next-door neighbor on Side 7.

Although still in her teens, Fra was already in charge of three young children—war orphans Kats Hoween, Rets Ko Huan, and Kika Kikamoto—the oldest of whom was nine. Because the children had refused to enter the local orphanage and insisted on staying with Fra, the officials involved had reluctantly granted her custody. With the war still raging, with her new situation and the need to earn a living, she abandoned a dream of becoming a fashion designer and decided to pursue a mechanic's license. Aware of her plight, some friends with connections helped her obtain work at the local military vehicle maintenance plant. Life on Luna II was hard but by no means miserable. She was young and resilient enough to recover when overworked, and her three young charges loved her as if she were their own mother.

"Fra! We brought you lunch!" Kika's high-pitched young voice echoed through the maintenance area where Fra worked. Over a dozen mechanics, most graying at the temples, crawled out from under the vehicles they were working on to greet her.

"Well," one worker said, "if it isn't little Kika again. We've been waiting for you, sweetie."

"Hey, Kika!" the foreman added, doffing his military helmet and wiping his brow. "What happened? You're three minutes early today!"

"Fra Bow works too hard for you guys," Kika retorted, sticking out her tongue. "She needs a break!"

Chuckling at her impudence, the workers in the plant gathered together, opened their lunch pails, and began eating.

"Kika, where are Kats and Rets?" Fra asked.

"They're coming. They're still playing Space Invaders."

"Well, tell them to get here on the double! It's time to eat."

"Roger Dodger!" Kika said, happily running off to fetch the others.

As Fra watched her little charge disappear, she realized how long the girl's pretty blond hair had become. She loved the sight of it and was even a little envious, but she also knew she should cut it soon. She reached into her purse and fished out a compact. It was military issue and utterly lacking in any aesthetic quality, but she nonetheless treasured it.

In the little mirror she saw grease smeared on her

cheeks. She took out a handkerchief and, while wiping them clean, resolved to buy some lipstick with her next month's paycheck. In the Force, Waves often scorned women who wore lipstick or makeup, but Fra didn't care. She was in her late teens, and she had rights of her own. She would do it for Amuro.

For Amuro. The moment the thought formed in her mind, tears welled in her eyes, and as she watched in the little compact mirror, they began rolling down her round cheeks. *Amuro.* She didn't care if he came back missing an arm or a leg or even if he fell in love with another woman. She just wanted him to come back alive. The thought grew louder and louder in her mind. If only he would survive. In the future he could make her cry or even make her angry, and she wouldn't mind. But if he died there would be no future. Only memories. And her last memory of him would be their brief exchange over a vid-phone as he departed from Luna II. That was a possibility she couldn't bear to think of. Fra again resolved to buy her lipstick. To buy it for Amuro. She slowly closed the lid on her compact.

"Hey, I was just about to break the three-thousand-point limit!" Rets complained to Kika as the two of them ran over to Fra. "Let's eat!" they yelled.

"Well, if you bring us lunch, you should at least be here on time," Fra gently scolded.

"Hey, it's Rets's fault," Kats whined, nonetheless taking out a paper napkin and wiping the hands of the younger two.

Noting Fra's face, Rets suddenly piped up. "You've been crying, haven't you?"

"Now, why would I do that, silly?" she answered, opening up the lunch rations the children had brought.

"Oh, no! Not *hamburgers* again," they all chimed.

"We're at war," Fra said, again in a scolding tone. "Think of all the poor soldiers out there who'd love to eat something as nice as this."

"You really think Zeon's that clever, eh?" Brite asked the pilots assembled on the *Pegasus II* bridge. "We've arrived at our rendezvous point ahead of schedule, so I say we ought to stay here till we can coordinate with the other fleets. The Corregidor shoal zone's an ideal place for us to hide."

"Well, the same's true for Zeon ships," Amuro answered. "Do you really think we can avoid being ambushed?"

"Why would they ambush us now? We're the only squad in the area, and the Zeon warships coming out of *Solomon* now are ignoring us. The archduchy wants to take on the entire armada, not just us. That's the way they think. And that means they don't want to waste a single ship on us."

"That's assuming a lot, skipper," Lieutenant Commander McVery said. The performance of the young MS pilots seemed to have impressed the veteran fighter pilot mightily, for he rested his arm on Amuro's shoulder and continued. "With all due respect for your own New Type potential, I disagree with your analysis, and I'm inclined to agree with young Amuro Rey on this one. Personally, I think there are enemy ships waiting for us."

"You really think an ambush is possible?" Brite said.

"You said it yourself, skipper," Hayato interrupted, speaking with far more conviction than usual. "We got here early. That'll bring the enemy out after us. Especially the Red Comet. I bet he wouldn't pass up an opportunity like this. I think we oughta get through the Corregidor area as fast as possible and then wait to coordinate our movements with the others.''

Brite finally caved in. ''All right, all right. Looks like nobody has an absolute majority here, but you've convinced me. I'll buy your ambush idea. We'll go through the shoals, but on one condition. McVery, I want you to agree to the lineup I've decided on.''

McVery grinned sheepishly and turned and looked at Amuro quizzically.

Amuro knew what was going on. ''The skipper's known us longer, sir,'' he said. ''And he's putting us out front.''

''Looks that way, doesn't it?'' McVery said.

''He's deferring to you in a way, sir. I'm sure you can understand. He knows you've already lost four of your men.''

''I know, *Mister* Amuro. 'Deferring' has a polite ring to it, but what it all boils down to is that the lieutenant doesn't trust me and my men.''

Amuro laughed. ''Sir, don't you think you're being a little too sensitive?''

''Hell, yeah. But in the Tomahawk Squadron we have to be sensitive. We have to be on our toes at all times.''

''I know what you're saying, sir. But I've gone up against the Elmeth once before, and I think it's better that I go up against it again.''

''All right. All right,'' McVery said. ''In front of you, my fair-haired lad, I'll skip the bravado.'' He gave Amuro's rear end a light slap, turned, and walked over to where his men were standing on the bridge, the magnets on the soles of his boots making a pleasant clicking sound.

Amuro shrugged his shoulders at McVery, turned toward Brite in the captain's seat, and saw Saila behind him. She had been watching his interchange with McVery and smiled.

Next, Brite formally announced the lineup. "Junior Grade Lieutenant Amuro Rey's G3, the Gun Cannons, and the GMs will lead the *Pegasus*. Lieutenant Commander McVery's Tomahawks will assume positions to our stern, starboard, and port. The *Cypress* and the *Greyden* will follow. And the four VX-76 Bowls will form our rear guard."

McVery made a forced smile and left the bridge, his men following without protest.

There was something about the way he handled himself that Amuro admired intensely. McVery had a masculine, charismatic quality that made men want to follow him. It involved principles and ideals, individual goals and a plan to attain them, and it all seemed like a mysterious art to Amuro. The only excuse he could think of for himself was his youthful inexperience, and the more he thought about that, the more inferior he felt. At least, he secretly prided himself, pretty blond Saila had finally introduced him into the ways of manhood.

That he could congratulate himself on such a simple matter in itself revealed his immaturity, for although youth does mature quickly through direct experience, a further test is the way experience itself is interpreted—whether it is glorified or accepted as a natural part of growing up. In Amuro's belief that his relationship with Saila had turned him into a more sophisticated adult and in his growing belief that nearly anyone could easily evolve into a New Type, he was still naive.

To the other four pilots in his Mobile Suit unit, Amuro announced, "Once we get through the Corregidor shoals, we'll be resupplied. We take off in an hour. I want everyone to go out there and do their duty.''

He tried to choose his words carefully but noticed that Kai and Hayato had smirks on their faces. They weren't deliberately trying to insult him, but he didn't like what he saw.

''Dismissed!'' he barked, immediately remembering he should have first asked them if they had any questions.

Kai Shiden, always the jokester, could not hold back a laugh. ''Hey, Amuro! You don't have to get so uppity just because you're our unit leader. We'll still respect you!''

Amuro ignored his friend's remark and turned on his heel. Why was he so tense? He wasn't experiencing a premonition or it would have manifested itself in a far more distinct manner. If this was just a new way to deal with precombat stress and anxiety, it wasn't doing him any good at all. If Kai, Hayato, and the others weren't there and if he hadn't been on duty, he would have liked to spend some time with Saila. But that wasn't possible now. The *Pegasus* was on a maximum combat footing and plunging straight into the Corregidor shoals.

Along with the other MS pilots, Amuro climbed into his Suit and performed a final check of his cockpit instrumentation. Then the face of Saila Mas appeared on his three-inch communication monitor.

''G3,'' she announced first. *''Junior Grade Lieutenant Amuro Rey. Are you ready?''*

''All systems are go,'' he replied over his mike. ''Currently at launch point.''

That was all Saila needed to hear, for her image immediately disappeared from his monitor. Faster than normal, it seemed. Was she deliberately ignoring him? Didn't women feel any special emotion at a time like this? He wondered. Then, in the next instant, he heard Petty Officer First Class Callahan Slay's high-pitched voice. *"G3! Stand by for launch! Ready . . . three . . . two . . . one . . ."*

"G3 now launching!"

The catapult mechanism beneath the Gundam's feet surged forward with a roar. He felt the *g* force, and a second later all man-made objects disappeared from view on his main screen and he found himself looking at a vista of millions of stars in a jet-black universe.

"C108! C109!" Over his receiver, Amuro heard the call signs of the other Mobile Suits behind him mixing with a rising level of static. The Gundam's autopilot system established the correct distance to precede the *Pegasus*, and the other Suits fell into formation. "Secondary combat speed," he called out.

He fixed his gaze on his main screen. A huge boulder soared toward him and then vanished to his rear. They were in the Corregidor shoal zone.

The Elmeth cockpit was roomier than that of a Zak, and Kusko rather enjoyed sitting in it, waiting. Her instrument panel glowed faintly in the darkness, and outside the only light she could see was that of the stars around her. With the sun out of sight, they seemed to be burning brighter than ever, densely matted in a world of black.

She saw the faint red shadow of Sha's Rik Dom next to her appear to drift slightly. *I wonder if he's noticed?* she thought, but decided not to dwell on it. In the weightlessness of space, it seemed absurd to position anything perfectly.

"The universe would be a lot nicer place if men weren't so power-hungry," she muttered to herself. She hated it when Sha and Sharia Bull started talking so righteously about the Zavi family and their own plans. It made her want to throw a monkey wrench into their schemes. She smiled at the thought. Perhaps, subconsciously, that was a reason she had taken a liking to Amuro Rey. It was not just because she had sensed New Type potential in him. She really had thought he was cute.

As if triggered by an association, she suddenly sensed something. With her right foot she gently pushed down on the activator pedal and aligned her Elmeth with Sha's Rik Dom. He seemed to have sensed something, too. Amid static, she could make out his fuzzy image on her communications monitor.

"Twelve o'clock, Kusko! Elevation zero!"

"Understood!" she replied curtly. She yanked back on the left and right steering levers, and the Elmeth rose steeply, bursting from its hiding place in the shoal zone. The six Rik Doms followed. Simultaneously, the *Madagascar* readied its cannon for attack.

Kusko gradually accelerated her Elmeth, cursing the men around her: "Politics, politics! They ought to think more about what it means to be a New Type!" Then she released the twelve remote-controlled Bit units carried in the Elmeth's fuselage.

As if on cue, beams began stabbing toward the Elmeth from in front of her. For a second Sha's Rik Dom was highlighted by the glare. *"Kusko!"* his voice barked over her speaker. *"Concentrate on operating the Bits! I'll cover you and the Elmeth!"*

"Thanks," she replied. She had registered the relative position of the Bits in her mind, and they were already charging forth toward the enemy she had visualized. Bits were configured with either a mega-particle cannon or a nuclear warhead and operated under a system of remote control that used brain waves amplified and projected by the psychom interface. Since Minovski particle interference had made radar-based guided weapons impractical, they were the only remote-controlled weaponry that worked effectively in space.

As Zeon and Federation forces converged at high speed, all thought of Amuro Rey disappeared from Kusko's mind. The twelve Bits headed for their targets, and their built-in video cameras recorded images that were amplified and projected by the psychom directly back to her brain, where they became an integral part of her vision. It wasn't hard to control the Bits. Humans easily recognize and act on visual information from multiple sources simultaneously—Kusko Al merely demonstrated this ability on a more advanced level, controlling the Bits through the psychom interface. There was a linear order to the visual information from each of the Bit units, and her cerebrum merely had to reflexively differentiate and exert control over it.

Then Kusko saw the Federation's Gundam model Mobile Suit.

In the same instant a suppressed thought barged into her consciousness. Was it really piloted by the young man she had found so attractive? By Amuro Rey? She had not really received any solid information to that effect, but she felt somehow certain it was he. And during her seconds of confusion one of her Bit units was destroyed. A light stabbed deep into her cerebrum, and she knew that the Gundam had taken a shot at her.

She swore. She knew if she had to confront the Gundam directly, she was in trouble. Her survival instincts—and the primeval fighting instincts that had qualified her for combat in the first place—would automatically assert themselves over all other thoughts. She began to feel pure hatred. For the Federation. For Zeon. For the war. For the male society that caused it. She was ready to fight.

As Sha watched, a rocket *whooshed* out of the Elmeth into the darkness, leaving a long trail from the blue-white cone of light billowing around its nozzle. It happened so abruptly that even he felt nervous. "Kusko!" he shouted into his microphone, pushing his red Rik Dom to catch up to the Elmeth. "Don't rush yourself!"

As if her action were the trigger, Sharia Bull led the other Suits forth, huge flares spewing from their skirted engine cowlings. Rik Dom engines were said to be equivalent in power to those of a cruiser. And at the same time the MS unit's mother ship, the *Madagascar*, sailed out from the shelter of a huge asteroid, firing both cannon and regular missiles in the anticipated direction of the enemy approach. The ship's huge Fife nuclear missiles, mounted both port and starboard, possessed such awesome destructive power that they had to be used before the opposing fleets of ships actually came into contact. Crewmen often claimed they could shake the whole universe, and when the first one launched, even the *Madagascar* seemed to shudder. In a blaze of light, the missile soared up past Sha and his men toward the enemy.

Amuro Rey intuitively sensed something coming straight for him. *Is this an auxiliary remote unit or an incoming missile?* he wondered. Suddenly his mind cleared, and he knew: *missile*! Unlike the leaping, relentlessly advancing impression generated by an Elmeth's remote units, missiles normally created a linear pressure in his consciousness and were thus easier to deal with. But if this were a missile, it felt unlike anything he had ever before experienced. It seemed to possess far more power.

He knew his comrades couldn't hear him, but he shouted out, "Kai! Hayato! Leave this one to me!" Then, lining up the sights on his beam rifle with the cross hairs on his main monitor, he shifted his aim 0.3 degree to the right. And in that instant several bursts of light erupted around his Gundam. Kai and Hayato had destroyed a couple of the attacking remote units from the Elmeth for him. He gave silent thanks and knew they were giving him time to concentrate completely on the incoming missile. And then he knew it was a Fife.

The first shot from his beam rifle hit home. The Fife exploded and mushroomed into a roiling inferno. The blast occurred in the middle of the two approaching fleets but was still powerful enough to make the Mobile Suit units of both forces shudder. The light from the explosion was sighted by Federation and Zeon warships several combat zones removed.

Furious, Amuro drove his Gundam forward toward the enemy at full speed, but as he did so, he saw the unique leaping light of several more Elmeth remote units bearing down on him from both sides. He wasn't in the mood to put up with any more attacks. He swung the Gundam fuselage left and right and fired two blasts from his beam rifle. Light from the exploding units streamed toward him, and he aimed the Gundam in a downward trajectory in their direction.

With a shock, he instinctively realized that whoever was piloting the Elmeth this time was even faster than Lala Sun had been. He was awed by the way the attacking units slid toward him and the way they timed the blasts of their mega-particle cannons. And he felt an intense mental pressure when they approached.

While Amuro had no way of knowing, the thought waves amplified by the Elmeth system's psychom interface had originated from Kusko Al's subconscious fighting instincts and were being projected in all directions. They appeared inside his own cerebrum like a moving black shadow, creating a powerful "force," a wall of sensation.

What is it? A chill suddenly ran down his spine.

At the same time Kusko Al yelled, "What's going on?"

Commander Garcia Dowal of the Flanagan Agency had once confidently told her, *"The Earth Federation putting New Types to real use? It's an utter fantasy. Don't worry about it. Ensign Lala Sun's Elmeth? That was just a prototype. It was pure coincidence the enemy attacked when the system hadn't been perfected yet, when she was in the middle of a test flight. She was killed in the line of duty, but it was an accident."* It was amazing, she realized, how different reality appeared to combatants on the front lines and theoreticians in the rear. Survival required an utterly different mentality from that of the desk jockeys. On the battlefield nothing was constant.

She had closed in on the Gundam enough to make out its form clearly. But to her horror, before she could get a good look, a force screamed through her mind. It wasn't light. It wasn't an audible voice. And it wasn't the force from a nearby explosion. But when it hit, it felt as though the skin and the hair on her head were being ripped off by a gale-force wind. It seemed like a hallucination, but it felt real. It *was* real. And it enabled her to avoid the next threat. She saw a light from the direction of the force and made her Elmeth soar upward just as several beams nearly zapped her from below.

She willed her seven remaining Bit units to attack the Gundam MS and at the same time aligned the sights of her Elmeth's twin mega-particle cannons. And then she saw Sha streak by her in his red Rik Dom. *Just in the nick of time*! she thought. Sha, too, began firing his bazooka at the Gundam, and a light from an explosion even greater than that of a Fife missile overwhelmed her main monitor.

She wondered if it was all over. *Was that Amuro?* she thought, feeling suddenly detached. If it was, well, that was that. *It's too bad, but it was your fault. You were shy and cute, but you treated me like dirt. If you were really the Gundam pilot, the slate's wiped clean now. There's something nice about that idea. We might have been together, but it just wasn't in the cards.*

But the battle was not over. Another powerful force roared through Kusko's mind. She opened her mouth wide and screamed.

"Kusko! Retreat!" She heard a voice loud and clear in the middle of the roar; it was her commander, Sha Aznable. *"Retreat!"* Without thinking twice, she put the Elmeth into reverse so suddenly that despite triple shock absorbers in the cockpit, the *g* force slammed her body toward the instrument panel in front of her. But she was well trained and never once took her eyes off her main screen.

Is that . . . is that really the Gundam? Her eyes widened. She could clearly see the enemy MS, illuminated by the light of an explosion, charging straight toward her, its gold-colored eyes flashing, glaring menacingly right at her, through her main monitor, through the sun visor on her Normal Suit.

In a simple twist of logic, her fear was canceled by rage. The mysterious pressure in her mind earlier had been like a shock wave, a form of mental rape that altered her thought patterns and rattled her psyche. And if such an unwanted, unpleasant sensation happened to have come from the Gundam, well, she was not about to forgive anyone. She turned the Elmeth's twin mega-particle cannons on the charging Suit and fired, but to her astonishment it skillfully dodged her attack with body English. Her chestnut hair practically stood on end as she screamed: *"It's a two-way street, Gundam! You tried to kill me. Now it's my turn! I'll turn you into dust!"*

Inside the Gundam, cold sweat beaded on Amuro Rey's brow and soaked his underwear. If he was going to be killed, he wished it could be under better conditions. The Elmeth quickly filled his field of vision, and each time it fired its cannons, he was surrounded by light from heat-emitting particles. That it was an oddly beautiful sight bothered him. It was absurd to feel beauty in something so deadly. He had no idea how he managed to avoid the beam blasts. He just knew that to escape from the force trying to envelope him—the force being projected at him from the Elmeth pilot through the psychom interface—he had to close in on the Elmeth itself. It was a realization that spurred him on, for with it and a little faith in his Suit, he knew he could survive the attacks.

"You won't be able to use the remote units this time!" he yelled inside his cockpit. He fired his beam rifle three times, and each time a powerful beam of light scorched through the blackness toward the Elmeth, but it "leapt" out of the way. He spun the Gundam fuselage, trying to keep on top of the weaving enemy machine, and in the process its metallic green image shifted from his left monitor to the main display. He was now directly opposite it. He pulled the trigger of his rifle and fired. The Elmeth started to swoop below him, but he had anticipated the maneuver and brought up the Gundam's left leg, smashing it into the Elmeth's prow. Under normal conditions what he had done would have appeared comical. His MS was humanoid, and he had in effect "kicked" the enemy. But his MS was also a weapon of war, to be used as he saw fit.

The shock of physical contact reverberated through the Gundam cockpit, and Amuro saw the Elmeth shudder. And in the same instant he felt a powerful "force" bearing down on him simultaneously from both his front and his rear. Could it be the Elmeth's remote units? Since he was attacking their mother machine, they were surely out to get him. In the force pressing on him he could detect a single thought: *Kill him!*

Could the pilot again be a woman? Several beams stabbed toward him from behind, but he anticipated them. Putting his Suit through an ear-grinding, bone-jarring maneuver, he managed to absorb the brunt of the attack directly with the shield in the Gundam's left hand.

WHOMP! The Gundam shook violently, and the impact nearly knocked him unconscious. He kept his eyes open but realized he hadn't been looking at his monitors or instrument panel. When he did, he saw glowing beams. And he saw an interaction among them—some sort of wave force controlling the beams. The waves created an undulating arc in space that quickly seemed to envelop the Gundam. He tried to scream but couldn't. His physical body wouldn't cooperate, and only an inaudible breathless cry erupted from the depths of his spirit.

The Vulcan cannon built into the Gundam's head belched and destroyed an incoming Bit carrying a nuclear-tipped missile. Both the Gundam and the Elmeth were swept along by the blast.

He cursed but kept his eyes open and again saw the flow of waves he had noticed earlier. He knew he was up against a formidable enemy. Staring straight at the Elmeth remote units weaving toward him, he fired three shots from his beam rifle. With the light from the earlier nuclear blast still illuminating the area, three more explosions occurred in a clump. The Gundam and the Elmeth were now locked in a close-range duel that quickly became a raging inferno. In a matter of seconds the battlefield was transformed from a conventional one, where isolated beams stabbed back and forth in the darkness, to a spectacular light show. The firepower was so awesome that to both Federation and Zeon warships in the area it looked as though not two machines but the entire Mobile Suit units of both forces had smashed into each other. Sharia Bull, with a direct view from the rear of the action, could only whisper in awe, "The Elmeth and the Gundam."

The two machines clashed again and again, and explosion after explosion occurred, but as with fencers in ancient times, whose supporters stood by and watched them duel to the death, none of the other Suits in the area at first dared intervene. Both the Zeon pilots in their Rik Doms and the Federation pilots in their Gun Cannons and GMs held back, perhaps fearing their Suits would be destroyed instantly if they jumped into the fray.

But Kai Shiden and Hayato Kobayashi knew what sort of battle Amuro was engaged in, and both had the same idea in mind—to make sure no one else interfered and thus give him time to dispose of the Elmeth. Taking the initiative, they boldly plunged ahead of the other Federation Suits, Kai yelling, "Don't let the fireworks distract you! More Zeon Suits are on their way—the ones with flared skirts!" Hayato gingerly maneuvered his Gun Cannon below the battle zone while Kai took the higher position. But someone had already snuck into the area.

As far as Sha Aznable was concerned, he was already too late. When a missile-bearing Bit unit took a direct hit from the Gundam, he was too close to the explosion and was temporarily disoriented as a result. *"Damn!"* he swore, reminded again of the frailty of human flesh compared to machines. Kusko Al was locked in close combat with the Gundam and appeared to be determined to destroy it at all costs, even if it meant her own destruction. Incredibly, she had even involved the remaining remote Bits in the close-in fray. The blasts from the particle cannon in the Elmeth were like screams of her frenzied fury.

"Kusko! Stay calm!" he yelled, training the sights of his beam bazooka on the Gundam. But he could not keep his aim steady. The enemy Suit, moving with blinding speed, was locked in a weird acrobatic dance with the Elmeth and two Bit units, firing beam blast after beam blast and giving him no room.

Sha then realized that he was witnessing what he had seen once before with Lala Sun, only this time the effect was even more powerful. It was as though the two combatants, their mutual wills locked in mortal combat, were exuding a force powerful enough to physically shut him out. Perhaps, he thought, it was because of the psychom interface. Perhaps it could not only amplify human will but even project it as a type of "power."

He knew he had no choice—he had to act to save Kusko even if it resulted in the destruction of the Elmeth itself. Beams from a Bit unit were already being deflected by the Gundam and striking the Elmeth. He had to get the Gundam away from her. He let the energy collect in his Rik Dom's beam bazooka. The Elmeth crossed in space above his trajectory. Then the Gundam. Then the two of them crisscrossed vertically at blinding speed. He fired and saw an explosion. He blinked, wondering if he had scored a direct hit, but then he saw the Gundam's smashed shield and watched the enemy Suit slide back behind the Elmeth. With a yell, he fired a second, then a third blast. The powerful verniers in his Rik Dom helped him twist and turn in space, and for a moment it looked as though the three machines—the Gundam, the Elmeth, and his own Rik Dom—would smash into each other.

The next moment Sha swore at his carelessness. The Gundam's left arm, which normally held a shield, reached over its shoulder toward its backpack beam saber hilt and swooped forward. In an instant a saber blade formed and connected directly with his Rik Dom's left leg. For half a second the Rik Dom and the Gundam were physically joined, but then the saber sliced into the leg like a sword into flesh and bone, particles from the beam exploding in light.

Sha groaned, his lips curling in an unvoiced curse. He lowered his beam bazooka and fired blindly at the Gundam, but it had already begun to move out of his line of fire, toward the rear of the Elmeth. Reluctantly, he eased off on his trigger finger and then heard a *WHOMP*! as an explosion thrust him upward. He looked up at the upper left instrument panel in his cockpit and to his dismay saw that an explosion had occurred in the damaged portion of his Rik Dom's leg. He had no choice but to disengage.

To his surprise, he also heard a strange ringing in his ears. He glanced at his main monitor and saw the light from another explosion fill the screen. *"Kusko!"* he yelled. He knew that the ringing in his ears was no ordinary ring, that Kusko had entered a state beyond his control, and that there was nothing more he could do. The ringing was also from the Gundam. There would be no retreat.

He began working feverishly to remove the Rik Dom's smashed leg from its socket.

Kusko Al's thoughts had already been infiltrated by Amuro's. Her hatred and rage had escalated to the point where she was doing far more than merely controlling the Elmeth's twin mega-particle cannons and Bit units. Nearly half her energy was radiating out into the vastness of open space like ripples spreading on the surface of a pond. But the accuracy of the three weapons she now controlled was increasing rather than decreasing. And they were all trained on the Gundam.

Amuro had to depend on the Gundam's new magnetic coating to help him evade the attacks, but the Gundam was still a mechanical system—a machine—and he knew there was a limit to its endurance. It simply was not capable of keeping up with the speed of human reflexes. And he knew the same was true of the Elmeth and its remote units. He projected an idea deep into Kusko Al's expanding wave of thought: <*If you want to stay alive, retreat!*>

Amuro's thought jolted Kusko with far more force than he would ever realize. She felt something bordering on physical pain deep in her head, and such an intense chill ran through her that she felt as though her brain matter would explode through her nose and eyes. The psychom, which normally amplified and projected her thoughts, was now working in reverse, receiving and amplifying Amuro's.

<*Retreat?*> she retorted, resisting his thought with all her might. And her thoughts were broadcast back to him.

And then Amuro knew at last. <Kusko! It's you, isn't it?> He remembered her chestnut hair and the seductive aura of her smile. But he was angry, his wrath triggered by a twisted sense of embarrassment. Why in the world should Kusko Al, of all people, be piloting the Elmeth? That question in turn triggered another, a lie, an attempt to hide his embarrassment: <I never wanted to sleep with you, you know!>

<You did!> she responded. <And you should have said so, boy. I would have said yes!>

The word "boy" caused Amuro to lose the final remnants of whatever self-control he had left. He screamed: <*"Boy"?* You think we're playing kid's games here? This is for *keeps*!> His beam saber sliced through the last surviving Bit unit, and the light from the explosion illuminated the Elmeth, its cockpit, and Kusko inside in her Normal Suit. Her smooth skin was covered in sweat, and she was trembling with fear, but to Amuro she seemed to be laughing at him.

<You're finished, Kusko!>

He sighted the Gundam's beam rifle on the front of the Elmeth, but then, to his shock, the same thing that had once happened in his confrontation with Lala Sun occurred again. With what felt like a physical force, he was jolted by a thought wave from Sha Aznable, trying to defend Kusko.

<*No, she's not finished, Gundam!*>

<Sha! Don't try to stop me! If you do, I'll have to kill you, too, just as your sister asked!>

<Artesia?>

<Get lost, Sha! Kusko's gone too far, and I've got a score to settle with her!>

Kusko Al had not laughed. She had merely lost control of her bladder and bowels and vomited against the sun visor of her helmet. Yet there was something she realized—that she could give herself to Amuro completely, unconditionally. It was both a powerful thought radiating out from her and a premonition of her own destruction. The enemy energy pulsing from Amuro had ripped her psychic sense of balance to shreds and left in its place an intense awareness of him as an individual.

<So it *was* you, wasn't it, Amuro?>

Thinking of him gave her a second of peace that transcended her earlier moments of sheer hatred. To rush madly forward with the Elmeth and die in battle with the Gundam began to seem absurd. It would be preferable somehow to take the passive route and let Amuro destroy her instantly with his beam rifle.

<Good-bye, Amuro!>

The same instant, a torrent of thought waves poured out of Amuro and the muzzle of the Gundam's beam rifle exploded in flame.

The same instant Kusko Al saw the flash and confronted her own death, Amuro saw a mysterious light flow from her. It appeared to be silver in color. And then he could hear her singing. Singing something about London . . . *London*, of all things.

<London Bridge is . . .
London Bridge is . . .
London Bridge is falling down
Falling down, falling down
London Bridge is falling down
My fair lady.
My . . . fair . . . lady . . .>

He heard a woman's voice overlaid on that of an infant. A beautiful woman. A "fair lady"? Could it be Kusko's mother? Then he heard an aria and a violin being played. Was it her father? The hand of a strong but gentle man touched the strings of the violin, saying, <Kusko, honey, that's not the way to do it. You're a half tone off. You've got to push down harder with your pinkie.> Her fingers ran up and down the neck of the violin. And Bach's *Air on a G String* formed a gentle curve and disappeared, wavering into the silver light.

<Build it up with wood and clay
Wood and clay, wood and clay
Build it up with wood and clay,
My fair lady. My . . . fair . . . lady.
My . . . fair . . . lady. . . .>

Then Amuro saw Kusko's pale fingers holding a pen and writing in a diary. He saw the letters she formed. They were distorted, and they, too, disappeared into the silver light, but he felt as if he had glimpsed her innermost, forbidden secrets.

<No! No! Stop!>

Kusko Al's gray pupils widened with terror and horror, and a young man's voice cried out, <I love you Kusko! I love you. You've got believe me!>

<No! No! Stay away from me, you filthy pig!>

<*London Bridge is falling down*
Falling down, falling down
London Bridge is falling down
My fair lady. My fair lady.>

<Stop! *Stop!*> It was almost a scream. And what Kusko Al saw, Amuro saw, too. A laughing man, apparently a Federation soldier, plunged a bayonet into the belly of her beautiful mother. Her father lay bludgeoned to death in a pool of blood.

<You *swine*!> As Kusko's scream spread out into the silver band of light and disappeared, Amuro again saw through her eyes, saw the face of the same Federation soldier, grinning, a cigarette clenched between his tar-stained teeth.

<*Build it up with wood and clay*
Wood and clay, wood and clay
Build it up with wood and clay,
My fair lady.
My fair lady.
My . . . fair . . . lady. . . .>

It was then that Amuro finally realized the enormity of what he had done—he had committed the unpardonable sin of killing someone he would normally have never dreamed of hurting. He had lost control to the war, the technology of machines . . . the whole situation. But it was no excuse. Kusko Al had been incinerated. It was too late. He wept and choked out the words, "Kusko, my fair lady . . ."

After the Elmeth exploded in a giant ball of light, the Zeon and Federation MS units finally closed in on each other in full combat, and the Federation ships—*Pegasus*, *Cypress*, and *Greyden*—began dueling with Zeon's Gattle fighter-bombers. It was an equal match in terms of firepower. The *Madagascar* was an attack battleship, and it and the Gattle squadron were not about to fall easy prey to anyone. Lieutenant Commander McVery and his six surviving Tomahawk fighters, for their part, braved the raging barrages and made a lightning strike on the enemy.

Meanwhile Amuro avoided two blasts from Sha's Rik Dom and unleashed a few rounds with his own Vulcan cannon, but then he was forced to start retreating from the area. The other Rik Doms were closing in on the *Pegasus*, and he had to stop them. But Sha was not about to let him.

<Why did you do it?>

As Sha charged toward him, leaping around some of the space debris in the area, Amuro finally regained his presence of mind. He knew the enemy Suits would have a hard time destroying the *Pegasus* on their own. If he turned around, he was confident he could take on Sha, but he knew Rik Doms were different from Zaks in terms of both speed and firepower. And he could feel Sha's own energy, targeted straight at him.

Over his receiver, Amuro thought he faintly heard a woman's voice somewhere crying, *"Sarkus! Sarkus!"* Had Sarkus McGovern, the GM pilot, been destroyed?

Then he heard a roar and a *wham* inside his cockpit. The beams used by the Rik Doms formed slowly and were so broad and powerful that even a near miss could make his Suit shake violently and throw off his sighting. But it wasn't a beam. Looking out from the Corregidor shoal area, he saw what appeared to be a large nuclear explosion in the distance.

And then he heard Sha Aznable saying, *<Is it true, Amuro?>*

Amuro was incredulous. Federation and Zeon MS pilots were battling to the death yet still were capable of "talking" to each other. Even in the midst of his duel to the death with Kusko Al, he had had verbal communication with her and had allowed a personal grudge to violate his belief that combat should always be depersonalized. His comment about Sha's sister had also been private, not the sort of thing one normally tossed at an enemy in the heat of combat. And he had no way of knowing how much his words had affected Sha.

<It's not possible to lie on this level, Sha! If you don't believe me, ask your sister!>

He had no way of knowing if Sha had received his thought, but the Rik Dom's remaining leg rose up and turned. Amuro fired his rifle. The blast went wild, and he aimed again. And then it happened. His beam rifle exploded in a flash of light.

Damn! he thought. Another, different Rik was coming at him, floating upward out of the darkness from below and to his right. Realizing it was trying to cut off his rear, he again put his Suit into retreat.

Lieutenant Commander McVery and three more of his Tomahawks never returned from their heroic mission. Nor did Ensign Sarkus McGovern in his GM. The *Greyden* was destroyed, as were four of the Bowl machines.

Back on the *Pegasus II*, Brite Noa looked up at the ship's screens at the expanse of the Corregidor shoals unfolding before him. "We took quite a beating," he muttered.

"But sir," Saila commented behind him, "at least we destroyed the Elmeth and three of the enemy's skirted Suits. And we annihilated the Gattle squadron and inflicted heavy damage on their warship."

"She's right, skipper," Mirai added, turning around while still manning the helm. "It was fifty-fifty. I'd say it was a draw and we held our own."

"And we collected quite a bit of data on Zeon's new Elmeth machine, sir," Mark commented, seated on the boom crane chair above Brite. "Don't you think," he continued, looking down at Hayato, "that for all intents and purposes we've wiped out half their New Type unit?"

"If Zeon has two or three more units like that one, the entire Federation's in big trouble. We wouldn't have been able to stop the Elmeth attack this time if it hadn't been for Amuro."

"I see your point," Brite said softly as he gazed at his crew.

When Amuro finally spoke, it was with bitterness. "No! That was Zeon's *only* New Type unit!"

Brite looked at him and frowned. "It's time for some

rest, pilot,'' he ordered. ''You'd better ask the medic for a tranquilizer.''

''Yessir . . .'' Amuro saluted. Then he turned around and asked Saila for the battle report. She walked over to him and handed him a large file. None of the other pilots were interested in it yet. They were simply happy to be alive, to have survived, and in groups of twos and threes they started filing out of the bridge area toward their quarters. Amuro, still holding the unopened file, watched his friends leave and then turned toward Saila.

''You knew the Red Comet was out there, didn't you?'' he said.

''I knew,'' she said. ''I could *see* him.''

''I told him what you asked. I think he understood.''

Without warning, Saila slapped Amuro across the cheek.

The *Pegasus II* and the *Cypress* rested briefly outside Corregidor. In a few hours the code words for the final attack on *Abowaku*—play the cemballo—would be signaled to the entire Federation armada.

This is the conclusion of *Escalation*, the second volume of the GUNDAM MOBILE SUIT series. Watch for the final volume—*Confrontation*—coming from Del Rey Books in February 1991!

ABOUT THE AUTHOR

Yoshiyuki Tomino is the creator of GUNDAM, beginning with the first animated television series in 1979 in Japan. Later he authored numerous novels using the characters he developed, as well as other film and television projects in the GUNDAM universe. He lives in Tokyo, Japan.

ABOUT THE TRANSLATOR

Frederik L. Schodt is a writer, translator, and interpreter based in San Francisco. A longtime fan of Japanese fantasy, he also likes robots—both imaginary and real. Among the books he has authored are *Manga! Manga! The World of Japanese Comics*, and *Inside the Robot Kingdom: Japan Mechatronics, and the Coming Robotopia* (Kodansha International, 1983 and 1988, respectively).